SUSAN PAGE DAVIS

TEA
TIN
PRESS

Chapter 1
1860

Iris was nervous the day Elder Whipple came home. He avoided looking directly at her when he greeted his family, then spent half an hour in the parlor with his wife, Louise, with the door closed. Iris could hear their low voices as she mixed the biscuit dough for supper, but she couldn't make out the words. The council had met for three days, and she wondered what decisions they had made for the community.

The Whipples' daughter-in-law, Annie, kept the churn going steadily on the other side of the kitchen. She and Iris worked in silence. No one spoke much at the Whipples' house. They just did their work.

Iris wished Annie were more talkative and friendly, but she always looked frightened and tired. When Iris spoke to her, she would answer with as few words as possible. Her husband, young John Whipple, was just as quiet. No one seemed happy here, and Iris thought it was the dry, bleak land that had drained them of life and joy.

Annie stopped churning, and in the brief silence, Iris heard the hum of Louise's flax wheel begin in the next room. The door to the parlor opened, and Elder Whipple stepped into the kitchen. Iris glanced at him, then turned her attention back to her work.

He walked over to her and stood for a moment, watching her knead more flour into the dough. "You'll be going to Brother Zale's place tomorrow," he said.

Iris found it suddenly hard to breathe. She looked up at his bearded face. His keen hazel eyes focused on her, not unkindly.

"I don't understand." Hadn't she pleased them here? She'd worked hard. She didn't want to be shuffled off to another family that might not treat her as well. She didn't know the Zales, and they might be farther from the mainstream of communication within the sprawling community of Saints, making it harder for Iris to seek out news of her own family.

The elder hesitated. "The men who went looking for your father's outfit returned yesterday. They didn't find any trace of them. It's been three months since your father's party set out, and nothing has been heard from them, Miss Perkins. The council is assuming the party is lost."

She let that sink in. "Lost?"

"Yes. That's the conclusion they've reached. It could be hostile Indians, or lack of water … It could be anything. The search party traced them about sixty miles southwest, but after that the ground was rocky. They didn't find any more evidence of a camp or anything like that."

She gulped and met his level gaze. "Or a struggle?"

"No. Nothing."

Iris nodded. It was so stark, so unsatisfying. This was her father they were talking about! Her brother, too. They had left with three other men at the end of May, to seek out ore deposits for the good of the community. Lead was needed, and iron, and of course anything more precious. They were to have reported back in a month, with a map of the places they had been, showing the location of any minerals or other features of interest to the Saints.

"The elders discussed the situation. We feel it's best if we send you to the Zale ranch."

Alarm ran through Iris afresh. "What for?"

"You need to be incorporated into a family, Miss Perkins."

"But I—" She hesitated, looking up at him cautiously. "Couldn't I stay here as part of this family, sir?"

He sighed. "The council feels it's time you were wed."

She caught her breath. "But my father—"

"Your father is likely dead, Miss Perkins. Others must make decisions for you now."

Iris tried to swallow the huge lump in her throat. The ache brought a mist of tears to her eyes. "Please. You mustn't— Oh, please don't do this. At least give them more time. They might have been delayed, or lost the trail, or gone farther than they anticipated if they were finding promising ore samples."

Elder Whipple shook his head regretfully. "I'm sorry. My wife and I would like to keep you on here, but it's impossible. Most young women your age have been married two or three years. It's your duty, my dear."

A gentleness crept into his tone at the last, and the heat of a flush crept up Iris's neck. She had often felt the elder's eyes upon her as she worked and had decided he meant no harm. He and Mrs. Whipple did insist that she put in long days, but everyone had to do that out here in the wilderness. It was necessary, and it was expected of all.

"I could serve you and Mrs. Whipple for a while longer." She glanced up at him with tentative hope, but he shook his head.

"I'm sorry. It's not possible."

Why not? She wanted to cry. But she held her peace. One didn't talk back to the elders.

But she couldn't help wondering. Was it possible Mrs. Whipple wanted her gone? Iris had scrupulously maintained a formality with her host and his son, so that no thoughts of impropriety could arise. Was her work not enough? She did far more than Mrs. Whipple each day. The older woman was worn out. She moved slowly and plugged away wearily at her housework and gardening. She didn't often smile, but occasionally she said to Iris, *Bless you, girl.* Once when Elder Treat and his wives came to visit, Iris had heard Mrs. Whipple say to the guests, *Praise God, we've got an extra pair of hands to help with the garden and the washing this summer.* Annie did her share, but she was slowing down now, too, with a baby coming in the late fall. Iris knew she could be a lot of help when the little one was born.

"I'll take you over there tomorrow," Mr. Whipple said. "It will take us all day in the wagon, so be ready at first light."

Iris nodded. Chore time had come, and he went out the door. Iris stood at the work table, kneading the dough longer than was recommended. She realized what she was doing and stopped abruptly, turning the dough out on the table. The biscuits would be heavy tonight, no doubt.

Chapter 2

Ed Sherman urged his horse stealthily forward in the cover of the scrub pines. He kept an eye on the band of feral horses grazing in a small mountain meadow below him, while continually scanning the brow of the opposite hill for a sign that his brother, Jake, was in position.

At last he saw Jake creeping forward on his blue roan gelding. The only bad thing was that the stallion leading the band of wild mares saw him, too.

Ed spurred his horse and broke from the cover of the tree line, urging his mount to charge down toward the black and white stallion. The wild horse snorted and squealed, turning immediately to prod his mares into flight.

Ed's horse tore toward them, and he guided his dun straight toward the stallion. Jake's roan pounded down the steep hillside opposite, approaching the pinto from an angle. Both brothers concentrated on the wily stallion. He didn't rear and paw the air or make a stand for his mares. He knew the men were after him, and he streaked for the safety of the mountains.

Ed kept after him, hoping to get close enough to throw a rope over the pinto's neck, but the stallion was much faster than Tramp, the dun Jake had chosen for him that morning from his string of horses. Tramp wasn't slow, but by comparison to the fleet stallion, he might as well have been one of the army mules Ed was forced to ride most of the time. Jake soon passed him, surging by on Spook, the huge blue roan. Ed had never seen any horse outrun Spook.

Until now.

Jake moved farther and farther ahead of Ed and the dun, but Ed knew it was hopeless. The pinto was gaining ground and heading for a steep upgrade. Spook made a valiant charge up it, but he tired soon under Jake's weight, and the wild stallion, as usual, leaped ahead unhindered.

Jake apparently saw the futility of wearing out his horse and risking serious injury on the rocky upgrade. He pulled Spook in, even though the roan was willing to continue the pursuit.

The stallion gained the high ground, then turned to look back at them defiantly from the hilltop. Only then did he rise on his hind feet and give a shrill, insolent cry of freedom.

Jake slumped in the saddle and turned Spook back down the hillside. No sense going on. They would never get close to him again today.

Ed sat waiting for his brother to reach him.

"No use," Jake said.

Ed shrugged. "We've got to corner him. There's no other way."

"Maybe if we could get Hal and a few other men from the fort, we could surround the whole band," Jake suggested, naming his best friend, Hal Coleman.

"Naw, the army's mounts are a bunch of plugs. Spook's the fastest horse in the territory, and even he can't catch him." Ed hated to admit it, but it was the truth.

"If that pinto was carrying the same weight Spook is, I'd have had him long ago." Jake took his hat off and wiped the sweat from his brow on his sleeve. "I think we're wasting our time, anyway."

"Oh, come on, he's so fast!" Ed leaned eagerly forward. "You could breed the fastest horses in Wyoming with him."

"He's ugly."

"No, he's not. He's colorful."

"His markings are pretty, I'll give you that," Jake said, "but his ears look like a mule's, and he's got a Roman nose. I want a horse that will sire colts I'll be proud of."

"Who cares if a horse is pretty, if he can do the job?"

Jake shook his head. "I'm looking down a long road, Edward. Right now I'm selling horses to the army. All right. Ten years from now, this country will be settled so thick there'll be towns and people who want good horses. Not just tough horses, but handsome horses, too."

"One of the mares was fine looking."

"I saw her," Jake acknowledged. "The bay with white stockings. Much nicer than most of these scruffy nags. She must have got loose from somewhere."

"She'd make a good brood mare," Ed said. "If she drops a colt from that stallion, could be he'll be pretty *and* fast."

Jake grunted, but Ed could see that the idea appealed to him.

"Well, there's not many decent stud horses in these parts," Ed said.

"You're telling me. That's why we're out here, isn't it? We must be crazy."

"The Mormons have some good horses," Ed said. He'd been into Utah twice now, on patrols the Saints had agreed to tolerate after the federal government's show of force three years earlier.

"*Nnn*, I'm not sure I want to start trading with the Saints. You hear all kinds of crazy things about them."

Ed looked up the hill to where the mustangs had disappeared. "Maybe next time we should forget about the stallion and go after that mare. She's probably bred, and she'd be easier to throw a rope on."

"I'll think about it." Jake glanced up at the sky. The sun was lowering toward the peaks in the west. "Come on. Laura will be waiting supper on us." He slapped his hat back on his head and looked around.

The mares had most likely regrouped to join up with their protective stallion again in the high country. Jake lifted his reins, and Spook immediately set out for home in a long, smooth canter. Ed didn't have to urge Tramp to follow.

Ed had been eating army rations for a couple of years now, and since he'd enlisted, he'd learned to take advantage of any opportunity to sit down to a home-cooked meal.

In some ways, he enjoyed life in the U.S. Cavalry, although the conditions were harsh. He'd always loved being out in the open air, and had fulfilled the old hankerings he'd had as a kid to see what was over the mountains.

The Green River Valley had seemed too small back then, and after both his parents were dead, he'd decided to enlist. His sisters had both married, and for a while Ed had Vivian's husband nearby and had gotten to know him. He'd hung around Fort Bridger, tagging after Lieutenant Josiah Hunt when he could. The Cavalry life had seemed the ultimate career to Ed. Horses, wide open spaces, an occasional skirmish with hostile Indians.

Then Josiah and Vivian moved east. Josiah had transferred to a regiment from New Jersey, his home state, and now there were rumors of a war between the North and the South. If the war had begun, Josiah could be anywhere now, right in the middle of things. Ed wondered if he hadn't ought to ask to be transferred back East, where he was apt to see action in this brewing new conflict. But the idea repelled him. Fighting Indians was one thing. Going up against men like himself was unthinkable.

And he was a bit homesick, if he admitted the truth. Jake was the only family member he had left besides Vivian and Jane, both of whom lived far away now. Jake was the only one who had stuck to the family homestead. He had no interest in being a soldier, although he did scout for the troops at Fort Bridger now and then.

No, Jake was more interested in raising horses at the ranch their father had started when they came west. And in the fall of '59, Jake had stunned everyone who knew him by marrying the daughter of the post commander.

Laura Byington Sherman was a wonder. Not only had she married his reticent brother, she had won the hearts of the entire garrison at Fort Bridger. She was kind and generous. She entertained

Ed and his friends whenever they could get away from the fort for an evening and ride the five miles to the Sherman ranch. She could ride like the wind. Spook was her horse, actually—a wedding gift from her father, the captain. She could shoot, too. Her father had taught her to use a rifle for her own safety, and Jake had trained her to use a revolver since their marriage.

And she was beautiful. Jake Sherman was the envy of every man west of Fort Laramie. Every trooper had despaired of being good enough to win Laura Byington's hand. The unmarried officers had buzzed around her, but she'd held them all laughingly at arm's length.

The corporate shock when she'd chosen Jake was enormous. Her unforeseen alliance with the quiet scout was the talk of the territory for months. None of Laura's suitors had ever considered Jake Sherman a rival. But Captain Byington seemed pleased with his daughter's choice, and Jake was obviously happy. Ed spent as much time at their house as he could.

Laura was waiting for them when they rode into the barnyard. She came eagerly from the barn with an expectant smile. "Where's that ornery stallion you boys were going to bring home?"

Jake grinned sheepishly and shrugged, his empty palms upward. "Halfway to South Pass."

She laughed, and her golden hair glinted in the sharp light of the falling sun. "You wouldn't be hungry, would you? I fed all the stock but these two poor critters you've been punishing all day. Put them away and come get something to eat."

Jake dismounted and scooped her into the crook of his arm. Ed couldn't hear the low words his brother murmured in Laura's ear, but he could see the supreme contentment that radiated from her as she squeezed him before turning toward the house.

Yes, Ed thought as he swung down from the dun's back, there was something powerful about marriage. It turned stolid, hardened men into kittens, and they loved it.

Chapter 3

It was still dark, with just a hint of increasing light, when Iris prepared to leave the Whipples' house the next morning. Her meager belongings were packed in a traveling bag her mother had stitched long ago of burlap, when the family had made the long journey west. Iris's memories of that harrowing journey were the tumbled, distorted recollections of childhood.

Her clothing and a few small items were all she had brought along when her father left on his mission and she came to stay with the Whipples. She wondered what would happen to the things they had left in the little house outside Salt Lake, the furniture and dishes that belonged to her parents. She didn't feel she should ask, but carefully bundled the items she could call her own into the bag.

Annie was in the kitchen earlier than usual. She was packing food in a basket by lamplight, and Iris knew it would be the lunch Elder and Mrs. Whipple would share with her on the journey. Louise Whipple had told her the evening before that she would accompany them, and Iris was glad.

A pot of coffee and a pan of cornmeal mush were simmering on the small wood stove. Annie glanced toward her and said, "Eat while you can. The elder is harnessing the team."

Iris took a tin plate from the shelf and spooned some cornmeal mush onto it. She didn't really feel like eating, but she knew she should. There was milk, warm from the cow, in an earthenware pitcher on the table, and she poured a little over the mush and sat down.

To her surprise, Annie took the molasses jug from the shelf and approached her. The sweetening was generally hoarded in the

Whipples' house. Iris was about to protest when Annie leaned close to her and whispered, "Be thankful you're going, girl."

Fear lanced through Iris. She looked toward the doorway and whispered, "Why do you say that? They're wedding me off against my will and my father's will."

"Yes, but not here," said Annie. "Pray that you'll be the first wife." She left the jug on the table and went back to her work.

Iris swallowed. She didn't touch the molasses jug. Perhaps Annie was offering it as a touch of parting kindness, but she didn't want to be blamed for using the precious commodity.

Annie's words ran over and over through her mind, but Iris didn't dare speak her thoughts aloud. Was that what had kept Elder and Mrs. Whipple closeted so long yesterday? Was it a choice of sending her off to the Zales or keeping her here as a sister wife for Annie, or even for Louise? Had Louise refused to allow that? She wished she knew what went on in the parlor.

She shivered and took her dishes to the worktable. A kettle of water was always kept heating on the back of the stove, and she dipped some into the wash basin. She wouldn't leave her dirty dishes for Annie to wash.

As she rinsed her plate the door opened, and John Whipple and his father came in from the yard.

"The wagon's ready," Elder Whipple said, and Iris nodded. "I'll tell the missus." The older man went up the stairs, and Iris dried her hands and went to the corner where she had left her bag.

John was eyeing Annie. "You all right?"

Annie nodded, but she sat down hard on a stool and sighed.

His mild concern was the closest Iris had ever seen him come to showing tenderness toward his wife. Iris hoped for Annie's sake that when the baby came Mrs. Whipple was on hand. If it happened while Annie was here alone with John, Iris doubted he'd be of much help.

Louise came down the steep stairs tying her bonnet strings. Her husband followed with a carpet bag in his hand. They were soon in the wagon. Elder and Mrs. Whipple sat on the seat, and Iris sat in the bed behind them, braced against the side of the wagon box between the luggage and the lunch basket.

Annie stood watching as they drove away, looking very forlorn, and Iris felt that perhaps her fear had made her miss a chance to make a friend. She lifted her hand in farewell. John was already striding toward the barn when they turned a corner in the dusty road and the farm was blocked from her view.

They stopped at midday to eat their lunch in silence. During the whole journey, the married couple barely spoke, and Iris felt vaguely that the Whipples were somehow cheating each other out of something good. While her own mother was alive, there was always talk and laughter in the Perkins house. But she had been away from that atmosphere so long that silence was beginning to seem normal. She helped Mrs. Whipple gather the dishes and wrappings into the basket without speaking.

The sun was far past its apex when they arrived at the Zales' ranch. Iris held on to the side board of the wagon as they creaked down into a hollow. They were close to the bottom of Echo Canyon, she thought, but she wasn't sure. They had gone east all morning, into the sun, away from Salt Lake and toward the Wasatch Mountains. The ranch was nestled in a dusty hollow in the foothills.

Row crops were maturing, but everything looked dry in the outlying fields. The hay and corn were somewhat stunted, smaller than what grew near the Whipples', but the heads of grain were forming. As they came nearer the unpainted house, things greened up a bit. Irrigation ditches cut through the gardens and a small wheat field. On one side was a large fenced pasture, and several horses snorted and trotted toward the fence to watch the wagon rattle down the road.

The house of weathered gray boards was built for practicality, not beauty. Two stories, square and boxy, it had glass-paned windows on either side of the front door, but the windows above had only shutters that opened and closed from inside. The barn was much bigger than the house and looked more substantial. Beyond it were a chicken coop, a corn crib, and a couple of small paddocks.

As Elder Whipple took the team into the dooryard, a black and buff dog came around the corner of the house and began barking. Iris's heart raced. This was her new home. She tried to reserve judgment, knowing that how she felt about this place would depend on the people who lived here.

A woman came slowly out the door and sent the dog slinking around the corner. She was nearly as old as Mrs. Whipple, with her graying hair caught up behind, and she moved stiffly, but welcomed them with a smile that was almost a grimace. Several children streamed through the door behind her and stood in a ragged row, staring at Iris. She saw one girl that she thought must be about fourteen, and her heart leaped. Company, perhaps, even if she was a few years younger than Iris. The others were of various ages, down to a toddler. A younger woman came out last, holding a baby against her shoulder.

"Mrs. Zale?" Elder Whipple asked the older woman.

"Yes, yes. 'Light and set for a spell, Elder. Brother Zale and the boys is out in the field, but I'll send one of the children for them." She looked around and said briskly, "Catherine, run for your papa now."

A girl of about eleven lifted her skirt without comment and hurried around the side of the house.

"This be Betsy," Mrs. Zale said, after the Whipples and Iris had climbed down from the wagon. Iris looked toward the teen-aged girl and smiled. Betsy looked toward her with a shy, almost fearful gaze. The corners of her mouth twitched, as if she would like to smile, but didn't quite dare.

Mrs. Zale nodded toward the other woman. "This be Delia, and her young'uns, Ezekiel, Liza, and the baby is Jonas. Come in, come in. Brother Zale and the boys will be in directly."

She led the way into the house. Elder Whipple lifted Iris's bag from the wagon and followed.

14

Iris swallowed hard. How would she fit into this large, grim-faced family? The girl Betsy was hanging back, waiting for the others to go in. When Iris approached the door behind the smaller children, she stepped forward.

"Welcome," Betsy whispered. She looked into Iris's eyes, then away.

"Thank you." Iris managed another smile.

"You're pretty," Betsy said.

"Oh, no."

"Yes. My father will be glad."

"Your father?" Iris gulped, not able to go on. Surely she wouldn't be forced to marry this girl's father? She remembered Annie's hasty words. *Pray that you'll be the first wife.* She glanced toward the doorway. The others were all moving through the kitchen, and she guessed that the adults would settle in the parlor.

"Is Delia—is she your—" Iris decided she couldn't ask what she really wanted to know and said quickly, her face reddening, "Is she your brother's wife?"

"No," Betsy whispered, looking nervously toward the door. "She be a sister wife to my mother."

Iris stared at her for a moment. It was not rare in these times, and she knew most of the elders and many of the other men practiced polygamy, but she hadn't known anyone well who was in that situation. She also knew the Washington-appointed governor hoped to see the practice abolished, but none of the Mormon men seemed to think that would happen in the near future. Not if they could help it.

"Betsy!" Delia came to the doorway. "Come help with the tea."

"Yes, ma'am."

Iris hauled in a deep breath and mounted the steps.

Chapter 4

"I know we can get that mare," Ed Sherman insisted.

His brother's skepticism was evident from the way he stayed slumped in his chair, sipping his coffee while Laura cleared the dishes from the breakfast table.

Ed was eager to go into the hills. He had talked Jake's friend, Hal Coleman, into giving up his day's leave to join the expedition. Hal had recently returned from a routine patrol into Arapaho territory and was ready to do anything that would take him away from the boredom of daily life at the fort. The two troopers, Ed and Hal, had arrived at the Sherman ranch while Jake was doing his early morning chores. It was harder than Ed expected to get Jake to agree to ride back up into the hills after the wild mustangs that had eluded him time after time.

"I dunno." Jake's apparent laziness was deceptive, Ed knew. His brother would spring into action once he was convinced they would succeed. He just didn't waste words or energy on enterprises he considered futile.

"What's so great about this mare?" Laura asked. She brought the coffee pot over and held it up. Ed shook his head and hoped Jake and Hal would refuse more coffee, but they didn't.

Ed sighed, wondering if he would ever pry Jake loose from the table.

"She's got good lines," Jake said with a slight shrug. "Edward thinks she'll drop a colt with the paint stallion's speed and the looks of a Thoroughbred."

"She's really something," Ed said. "She may even have had her foal by now."

Jake frowned. "You don't even know for sure there was a foal in question."

"Half the mares had colts beside them the last time we were up there," Ed reminded him. But it had been several weeks since they had tried to trap the stallion. Summer was nearly over, and the regular foaling season was past, Ed knew.

"Maybe next year," Jake said.

"If you think we can do it, I say let's give it a try," Hal Coleman said. He was wearing a cotton uniform blouse and threadbare light blue regulation pants. It was far too warm for the uniform jacket, and he'd long since rejected the hat issued to him in favor of a felt slouch hat. Ed, on the other hand, had reverted to the comfortable civilian clothes he had available at his brother's house.

"Even with three of us, I don't know if we can do it," Jake said. "We need a canyon or someplace where we can box them in."

"We can do it," Ed said, his fervor sparking once more. "Old Paint Bucket will think we're after him again, and we'll just let him hoof it while we take after that mare."

Laura laughed. "I'd like to see the brilliant animal that has you two buffaloed. I wouldn't have thought any horse could outrun or outthink the Sherman brothers."

"I'd like to see him, too," Hal said. "If half what Ed tells me is true, he's quite a horse."

Jake curled his upper lip. "Crafty and quick, but I'm not sure he's what I want for my breeding operation."

"Let's just go for the mare then." Ed leaned forward eagerly. "Let the stud run all he wants, we're going for that mare. You know she's a beauty."

Jake eyed him through his lowered lashes. "You think I've got nothing better to do, don't you?"

Hal drained his coffee cup and leaned back. "Jake, if you just want to stick around home today and split wood, I'd be honored to help you."

Jake smiled at him. "Now that was spoken like a southern gentleman and a true friend. You know you're bustin' to get into those hills and chase wild horses. You been looking at nothing but mules and plow horses for months, am I right?"

"Something like that." Hal's usual assignment was the care of the fort's remounts, and while the officers rode horses and often arrived with their personal mounts, the enlisted men for the most part drew mules from army's remuda. Hal was always on the lookout for replacement animals, but they were hard to come by out here, and in the spring Captain Byington had sent him all the way to Fort Laramie for a dozen remounts.

"Maybe you could catch a mare or two for the army," Laura said, her blue eyes snapping with humor.

"That's all I need," Hal said. "Wild horses to train. But I'd love to help you get one, Jake."

"How's that sorrel you're riding?" Jake asked, and Ed sat up with a muffled whoop.

"I picked the fastest thing we got," Hal said, his Georgia drawl creeping out just a bit. "Belonged to a lieutenant who met his demise last winter, and the captain sent his folks some money and told me to add the horse to the string for the officers. I got permission to give him a little exercise today."

Jake laughed, but Laura's surprise was obvious. "Why didn't Father just buy him for himself? He could use another good horse."

Hal shook his head. "The captain is a scrupulous man, and he doesn't want anyone saying he profited from something like that."

"How about you, Ed?" Jake asked. "You want to ride Tramp again?"

"Sure, unless you've got something faster."

"That's assuming my wife won't mind me giving Spook a chance to stretch his legs." Jake turned toward Laura, the owner of the big blue roan.

"Of course." She gathered the cups, but her disappointment showed in her tiny frown, and Jake reached out and touched her sleeve as she turned away from the table. "Should have told me you wanted to go, sweetheart."

"I didn't think you'd let me."

Jake stood up laughing. "Put your riding duds on. I'll use Shakespeare today."

"No, you take Spook," Laura said quickly. "You know I can't rope anything that's moving. You need to have the fastest horse, so you can get in close and drop a loop on that mare for certain."

Jake leaned toward her and dropped a light kiss on her lips. "Fine, then, I'll put your saddle on Shakespeare." Jake's usual saddle mount, Shakespeare was a sturdy, reliable bay, but not a racehorse.

She ran eagerly to the bedroom and closed the door. Ed couldn't stand another moment's delay. "Come on, let's go get the horses ready."

"You got yourself a wonderful woman," Hal said to Jake as he pushed his chair back.

Jake grinned as they headed for the barn. "She's right, you know. Not only does she have the fastest horse in the territory, but she can ride like anything, and she keeps house like an angel, but she can't rope worth beans."

Chapter 5

The work at the Zale ranch was grueling, and Iris was immersed in it the day after she arrived. The Whipples were leaving immediately after an early breakfast. Before they drove out in the dawn, Eleanor Zale handed her an apron and a paring knife.

Blisters swelled out on Iris's fingers after an hour of peeling vegetables, but when she moved on to the next task, she realized food preparation had been easy, compared to this. At least she had been able to sit on a stool while she peeled. Now she stood hunched over a tub of tepid water, scrubbing little Liza and Jonas's soiled diapers on a washboard. At the Whipples' there had been no babies yet, with smelly clouts to keep clean. Wash day had come once a week there, but she got the unmistakable impression that it was an almost daily chore at the Zales'.

Betsy and Catherine came to help her hang out the clean clothes late in the morning. Iris smiled wearily as Betsy took one handle of the big basket and helped drag it to the clotheslines behind the house. The blisters on her hands had broken open, and the strong soap had gotten into the sores, causing severe pain.

"Thanks."

Betsy nodded but said nothing. She and Catherine bent to the work, and Iris was glad for that. The Zale girls seemed to know that shirking would not be tolerated.

"Well, this is better than picking beans all morning," Catherine muttered, and Iris laughed.

The two girls stared at her with wide, startled eyes.

"You're right, it is better," Iris said. She seized a diminutive dress of Liza's and stretched her arms up to grasp the clothesline that swayed in the constant breeze. "What else do you girls do?"

Catherine and Betsy looked at each other, then Betsy said hesitantly, "Everything. We feed the pigs and the hens, gather eggs, tote water and wood, wash dishes, help make jam and preserves, sweep and scrub and—well, just everything."

"And watch Delia's brats."

"Catherine!" Betsy sounded truly shocked at her sister's outspokenness in front of the stranger. She turned quickly to Iris, in a seeming effort to cover Catherine's rudeness. "The little ones can be trying."

"They're your sister and brothers," Iris said, still not certain of the family's configuration.

"Half," Catherine said bitterly, looking over her shoulder toward the house. "Since Pa decided to enter celestial marriage—"

"Hush!" Betsy hissed. "You mustn't talk about it."

"It's made Mama old and mean." Catherine's voice broke a little as she spoke the defiant words.

Iris looked at them helplessly. If she were Catherine's sister, she would put her arms around her and offer what comfort she could, but Betsy stood stiff, as though she couldn't move.

"Pa will punish you if you say such things," Betsy said between her clenched teeth.

Tears swam in Catherine's brown eyes, and Iris couldn't stand still any longer. She threw the clothespin she was holding into the basket and stepped toward Catherine.

"Here." She wrapped her arms around the younger girl and stroked her hair. "You've got me now."

"That's right," Betsy whispered with thinly disguised rancor. "We've got you, too, now."

"What do you mean?"

"You'll be lording it over us like Delia, like as not." Betsy wouldn't meet her eyes when she said that, and Iris drew a quick breath.

"Are you saying I'll marry your pa and be … "

"No, not Pa," Catherine said. She raised her head, but didn't step out of Iris's embrace. "You're scaring her, Betsy!"

"Not Pa," Betsy agreed. "I'm sorry. I didn't mean to make you think that. That would absolutely kill Mama. Didn't they tell you?"

Iris shook her head, almost afraid to hear what was coming.

"It's Rufus," said Catherine. "He's your intended."

"Our big brother," Betsy explained.

Iris nodded. She had met Rufus the night before and sat across from him at the supper table, trying to ignore his slovenly table manners. And he had sat in the parlor with the Zales and the Whipples while they held a stilted conversation. Louise Whipple had gotten Eleanor Zale to detail her recipe for sour pickles, and that had eased the strained atmosphere for a few minutes. The men began to discuss livestock. Then Eleanor asked Delia about her little ones, and Delia had gushed on about her darlings for a good twenty minutes, describing three-year-old Ezekiel's clever sayings and baby Jonas's progress in making the transition to solid foods. It was as if she'd yearned for an audience for years and had finally found an outlet for her pent-up pride.

Rufus had sat in a corner, staring down at the drab hand woven carpet, saying nothing the whole time, except when his father or Elder Whipple spoke directly to him. Iris thought him quite a dolt. Even quiet John Whipple, Annie's husband, was more attractive than Rufus.

"Did your ewes produce well this year?" Elder Whipple had asked him.

Rufus stirred himself and shrugged. "Middlin'."

Iris was repelled by him. His broad, bovine face held a stupid, vacant expression. He was large of frame, like his father, and no doubt his strength was an asset to the ranch. His red hair warned of a quick temper, but his dull eyes told her he hadn't much wit. In fact, as she had looked around the parlor, the Whipples' faces showed more mental quickness than any of the others in the room, with the possible exception of Brother Zale.

Iris felt him looking at her, and when she glanced toward him, she inadvertently flinched. Isaac Zale's gaze rested on her with a calculating glitter, and at that moment she had remembered with a chill Betsy's first words to her—*my father will be glad.* At that moment in the parlor, a terror had gripped her, and she had avoided looking at Brother Zale again, all through that tortuous conversation and the family devotions that followed.

Even now, in the bright sunlight and with none of the Zale men in sight, she was still afraid of Isaac Zale. The memory of his dark, shrewd eyes on her did a curious thing. It made the concept of marrying the oxlike Rufus less impossible to consider.

Chapter 6

Patience was never one of Laura's virtues. She waited the agreed upon time astride Shakespeare, until she was certain the three men were in position, then she edged the bay forward to where she could see the mares. Their flowing tails switched back and forth, keeping the flies off while they grazed. The grass was poor this late in the season, and she wondered how they would get by in the winter ahead. Perhaps they would leave the mountains for lower ground with a milder climate.

The stallion, marked with distinct black and white blotches, trotted around the small band, snorting and snatching an occasional mouthful of grass. Four of the seven mares had foals at their sides, thin, gangly little things. Laura almost laughed as she watched them skip around the small clearing, then return to their mothers for a quick drink of milk. Shakespeare shook his head and pulled at the bit.

"Easy," Laura whispered. "Please don't make a sound, fella."

She saw the mare Jake wanted then. Her dark brown coat was glossy, like Laura's mother's walnut table. Her black tail swung long and full, and Laura waited, wanting to see the mare raise her head. From what she could tell, the horse's head was finely chiseled, her ears delicate and expressive. At last the bay turned a little, and Laura saw that she was heavy, her sides distended unnaturally. Ed was right! She was with foal, even though it was long past the season. It would be hard on the little one, being born so late in the year in this harsh territory.

Suddenly the wary stallion lifted his chin and froze, his black ears pointing straight toward Laura. She knew she was downwind of him. Had she or Shakespeare moved so much that he spotted them, even though they were still shielded by the stunted pine trees? Or had he heard Shakespeare's eager fidgeting?

She held her breath. The stallion snorted and swiveled on his hind feet, this time staring toward the hillside behind him. Laura caught a flicker of movement, then Jake and Hal burst from cover on their mounts, and Ed urged Tramp out from farther down the little valley. She felt Shakespeare tense, and she let him bunch up beneath her.

"Go!" she said softly, and the usually placid gelding hurled himself into the clearing.

It was her job to chase the stallion and get him away from the mares while the Sherman brothers and Hal Coleman went after the bay. They had all agreed that, no matter what, they would let the stallion go and concentrate on the bay mare.

Laura charged toward the paint stallion, and he whinnied, an ear-splitting cry that echoed from the sides of the little valley. Shakespeare seemed to have second thoughts and hesitated just a fraction of a second, so Laura let out a yell and dug in her heels.

They ran straight for the paint, and for an instant she thought he wouldn't move, but would stand there waiting to do battle with Shakespeare. His low call was a warning, and Shakespeare faltered. Laura felt something she seldom encountered—a rush of fear. The stallion was bigger and meaner than Shakespeare, and he had no loyalties or conscience. He bared his teeth and snorted again, then lunged toward her.

Suddenly a grayish blur rushed past on her right side—Jake dashing in on Spook.

Spook charged at the stallion, and the paint reared up, then hit the earth again on all fours. He dodged around the big roan and tore past Laura, down the valley after his fleeing mares.

Laura whirled Shakespeare in despair. The stallion was smarter than they'd bargained on him being and hadn't run from her. He knew the odds were greater today, and something was different. He was set on defending his band.

26

But the diversion she and Jake caused had given Hal and Ed enough time to separate the bay mare from the rest of the horses. They had chased her up a hillside, and as the stallion made good his escape behind the other six mares and the four foals, the two men pursued the lone mare up a steep slope, toward some tumbled rocks. Both men were swinging their ropes in big loops above their heads.

Laura pulled Shakespeare to a stop, knowing she couldn't reach them in time to be any help. No sense tiring him out. As she watched, Ed's rope snaked out, but the mare dodged and the rope fell useless to earth.

"You all right?" Jake called, and she nodded.

Jake spurred Spook toward the other riders then, leaving Laura and Shakespeare behind. Spook bolted across the grass and up the hillside. Laura held Shakespeare steady and watched in silent wonder as Jake bore down on the other horses. His rope glided out swift and true and settled around the lovely mare's neck. She stopped then and stood trembling, her sides heaving. Ed moved in closer and tossed his rope over her head, too.

Laura resumed breathing then and rode at a leisurely trot to meet them at the bottom of the hill.

"Jake's got a gift," Hal said, grinning at Laura.

"He's feeling pretty good right now, aren't you, Jake?" Ed said. "I've got to practice my roping more."

The brothers walked Spook and Tramp slowly down the valley with the mare between them. She seemed almost docile, not fretting or fighting, and Laura concurred with Jake's opinion that she hadn't been in the wild as long as the others.

"Good job," she said as she brought Shakespeare alongside Spook.

"Where were you at the start?" Ed asked his brother with a grin. "I thought you'd left me and Hal to do the job alone."

"Don't fuss at him," said Laura. "If Jake hadn't come after me, I might be piccalilli by now. That old Paint Bucket was not going to let me chase him away. I thought for a second there he was going to bash poor Shakespeare's brains out."

"I guess Shakespeare doesn't have a very commanding presence," Jake said with a laugh. "Sorry, but when I saw that stud make like he was going to fight, I needed to distract him from Laura more than I needed to help you run down that mare."

"You're right," Hal said. "Catching a horse isn't worth getting hurt."

Jake motioned for Laura to bring Shakespeare up close beside Spook. "You sure you're all right?"

She nodded. "Nothing wrong with me, I told you. I didn't help much, though."

"Yes, you did. You kept him away from us just long enough."

"We couldn't have done it without you," Ed said, but Laura thought he was being generous.

"Well, this old girl couldn't run too fast, today, anyway, by the look of things," Hal said, eyeing the mare closely.

"She's going to foal any time," Jake agreed. "Let's get her home, nice and easy." He looked at Laura again. "If it's a filly, sweetheart, she's yours."

Hal laughed. "What if it's a raw-boned stud colt you don't want seen on your ranch, Jake?"

"Then I'll make a present of him to the Cavalry," Jake said.

Ed huffed a protest. "That colt is going to be the sweetest thing you ever seen."

"Saw," said Jake.

"Right."

When they reached the Sherman ranch it was late afternoon. Jake opened the corral gate and released the mare inside.

"I'd better get some straw down in the big stall," he said, watching the mare sniff around the inside edge of the high fence. "She'll foal by morning, or I miss my guess."

"I'll help you," Hal said.

Laura swung her leg over the saddle and dismounted.

"Here, let me take care of Shakespeare." Jake reached for Laura's reins.

"You're such a gentleman." She relinquished them with a smile. "I know you're just putting my horse away so I can get into the kitchen faster."

"You bet."

Laura laughed. "Dinner in thirty minutes, gentlemen."

As she turned away, she heard Jake say, "I don't know, Hal, that gal can just about ride circles around me, but there's times—"

"How close was it?"

"Scared me a mite. Scared her, too, I think."

Laura lingered just long enough to hear Hal's quiet answer.

"You were there when she needed you, Jake Just do whatever she'll let you do to take care of her, and thank God you've got her."

Chapter 7

It was late September, and Iris considered herself lucky. She had toiled for the Zales for nearly a month, and nothing more had been said of her upcoming nuptials. She took her orders each morning from Eleanor, and later in the day got revised ones from Delia. She tried her best to fulfill both women's wishes, but it was tiring, thankless drudgery. She thought wistfully of the Whipples' farm and wondered if Annie had given birth yet, and if the Whipples had a grandson or a granddaughter. She would gladly have returned to them as a servant, to wash the baby's clothes and cook and clean unpaid.

Instead she slaved for the Zales. Betsy and Catherine continued their tenuous friendship with her, but Iris knew she couldn't count on them for support if anything went against her. Their father ruled the entire family with a heavy hand. At least he and the older boys, Rufus and Luke, and sometimes even nine-year-old Elmer, were away from the house nearly all day.

It was the busiest time of year on a farm. The men had crops and livestock to tend. Iris spent long hours helping the women, Betsy, and Catherine preserve the produce from the garden. This was their lot for late summer and autumn; Iris understood that. The washing and mending never ended, and of course the cooking and cleaning. Spinning, sewing, and weaving were winter chores for the women, and she found herself longing for those evenings when she could sit down with a needle and thimble, instead of being on her feet for such interminable hours, working on and on until the sun set.

Usually she managed to stay busy during the time when the men ate breakfast. Some days they took their noon meal at home, but more often Delia and Iris packed it for them in the morning, and they took it with them to whatever part of the ranch they were working at that day. They were nearly always home for supper, though, and the family ate together.

At those meals, Rufus sat hunched over his plate. At first he concentrated on getting as much food into his stomach as he could, it seemed to Iris. She tried not to look at him, as he tended to pick up meat bones with his thick fingers, and without fail he chewed with his mouth open.

Once he'd downed his first helpings of supper, he generally began to turn his attention elsewhere as he reloaded his plate, and Iris could feel him watching her.

One night Brother Zale had looked down the table at her and asked suddenly, "Well, Miss Perkins, you've been with us three weeks now. What do you think of the Zale family?"

Iris was startled speechless. As she cast about for an appropriate but truthful response, she began to panic. "I—well—it's a large one, sir."

Brother Zale laughed heartily, as though she had said something extremely witty, and Rufus looked at his father, then guffawed. The younger children began to giggle nervously, and soon everyone was laughing except the two Mrs. Zales.

"Yes, it is large, isn't it?" Brother Zale said with more than a touch of pride. "So large that we need more space."

Iris made sure she was never alone with Rufus, and he said little to her, but he stared at her. Only once had she come face to face with him when no one else was nearby. She was sent to the garden for vegetables for supper, and as she went through the back yard, she saw that Rufus was there, fitting a new handle to an ax. She hoped he was engrossed enough in the task not to notice her.

As she passed, he said, "Howdy."

"Howdy." She kept walking, not looking at him, but she heard him lumber to his feet behind her.

"Hey! I'm talking to you!"

She quickened her steps and reached the edge of the garden.

She pulled carrots quickly and filled her basket in record time, then straightened. Rufus was waiting as she stepped over the rows of root crops.

"You never talk to me." The sun was behind him, and Iris squinted. He stood with his feet slightly spread and the ax in his hands.

She swallowed hard. "I barely know you."

"You live here."

"Yes."

"You been here some time."

"Yes."

His eyes narrowed. "I'm going to marry you. You know that, don't you?"

Her heart pounded, and she took a deep breath. Elder Whipple had told her she was to be married. The Zale children had said Rufus was her appointed bridegroom, but that was all. No adult had told her officially what her future would be.

"No one has told me anything. I—I didn't know but I was here to help your mother and Delia."

He looked her up and down, and she squirmed. "That's a nice dress," he said softly. He took a step toward her, letting the axe fall, and Iris pushed past him.

"Hey!" he cried.

"Your mother needs these carrots." She flung the words over her shoulder, in hopes that he would respect her need to obey his mother.

After that, Rufus watched her even more. When he came in from milking in the morning for his breakfast, he gaped at her. Iris tried to have the breakfast table ready early, and to find an errand in another part of the house when the men came from the barn. When she couldn't get away, he would grimace at her and say, "'Morning." She supposed he thought it was an attractive smile. Under the

33

piercing eyes of Brother Zale and Eleanor, Iris forced herself to be civil to Rufus and return his greeting with a neutral "Good morning."

When the last of the fodder for the animals was put in for winter, Isaac Zale and his sons began working at the sawmill every day, and a pile of lumber began to rise behind the house. Iris did not ask what it meant, but the children told her.

"That's your new house," Elmer said one day, watching her face to see how she would react.

Iris was helping Elmer and Catherine clean out the chicken coop, and it was a smelly, filthy job.

"My house?" Iris asked, her heart tripping.

"Not a house," Catherine said with superiority. "Pa's building a new room on for you and Rufus, and another room for Delia's brood."

Iris sneezed at the dust Elmer raised, pitching soiled straw outside.

"You don't know what you're talking about," Elmer sneered.

"Do so," said Catherine. "Delia's increasing again."

Iris shot a glance at Elmer, but he seemed oblivious to the implication. "So what?"

"So she needs more room. She doesn't want her children mixing with us all the time. She wants Pa to give her her own parlor, too."

"You're lying. The new house is for Rufus and Iris," Elmer insisted belligerently.

Catherine shrugged. "You're just ignorant, Elmer Zale."

"Henry and Priscilla got their own house," Elmer said. Henry was their oldest brother, who was married. He'd been sent down into southern Utah, Iris had learned from scraps of conversation between the family's women. He and his wife and young daughter were living in a new community the Saints had started there.

"Well Rufus is staying here. I heard Pa say that he had to stay and help him with the ranch unless the elders make him go someplace else."

34

Iris sneezed again. "I'm going outside and start moving the litter to the manure pile."

The two children didn't protest, and she went out into the barnyard and began wielding a dung fork, wondering when the news would be broken to her officially, and how much time she had.

The thought of wedding Rufus nauseated her now, and she had to remind herself that this lot was better than that drawn by many women in Utah.

There had been no news of her father and Conrad. On the rare occasions when a visitor rode into the Zales' yard she hoped for word, but none came. She was seldom permitted to speak to outsiders. Eleanor or Delia dealt with them if Isaac was away from the house. She heard nothing from the Whipples or the people she had known when her family lived closer to Salt Lake. Iris began to wonder whether the Zales would even tell her if news came.

What if her father and Conrad had come back, and she was gone? What if they tried to trace her, but no one would tell them where she was? The elders had made the decision that she was to be Rufus Zale's wife. Would they allow her father to protest that ruling?

That's crazy, she told herself. *Don't panic. After all, God knows where you are.*

But she was not comforted by that thought. So far God had not given her any reason to hope. A keen desperation drove her through her chores.

It was just before supper that she was told. Betsy was setting the table while Iris helped Eleanor take up the food for the meal.

"Betsy, go help Delia with the children," Eleanor said.

Betsy paused, then set down the handful of forks she held without a word, leaving them on the table.

When the girl had left the room, Eleanor said, "You and my son will wed in ten days."

Iris swallowed hard. "Yes, ma'am."

"After devotions, you will be allowed to sit with Rufus in the parlor."

35

"T-tonight?" Iris whispered.

"Tonight and every night."

Iris shuddered. "How long?"

"Until the wedding."

"No, how long must I sit with him each evening?"

Eleanor opened the oven door and began spearing the baked potatoes with a fork, piling them in a wooden bowl. "Goodness, child, what does it matter?"

"It matters to me, ma'am. I should like to know."

For the first time, Eleanor looked slightly embarrassed.

"I don't know. Half an hour, perhaps?"

"Thank you."

Iris went to the table and picked up the forks. Numbly she began putting them into place.

"I'll call Brother Zale and the children," Eleanor said, and Iris had a brief moment alone to compose herself before the family descended.

Chapter 8

"It's a filly." Ed's sharp disappointment surprised him. He hadn't known how much he'd hoped the foal would be a colt, as swift and proud as his sire.

"She's a beauty," Laura said softly, her eyes shining. The paint stallion's colors were splashed liberally over the baby's woolly coat, and her velvety muzzle and broad brow were as finely shaped as the mare's.

"No doubt who her daddy is," Ed said.

Jake slipped his arm around Laura's waist as they stood looking into the foaling stall. "You've got yourself a fine looking filly, Mrs. Sherman."

Laura laughed. "I'm happy with Spook, thank you."

"Spook won't last forever."

Ed frowned at his brother. Sometimes Jake's stark practicality was a bit blunt.

"By the time Jake has this one trained for you, you might be ready for another mount," he suggested.

Laura reached out and stroked the mare's nose. The horse snuffled and shuddered, but she didn't pull away.

"She's got to be a Thoroughbred."

"Could be," Jake said.

"What will you do if you hear someone lost her?" Ed asked.

Jake shrugged. "Anytime someone loses livestock in this area, we usually hear about it, or at least they hear about it at the fort."

Laura nodded. "You should ask around, Ed. But even so, you boys earned her."

Ed pulled in a deep breath. The horse belonged to Jake, there was no question of that, but it felt good to know he'd helped his brother catch her.

"At least we know she's a fine brood mare," he said. "Couldn't ask for a sweeter little filly."

Jake nodded. "Yup. I make her to be about five years old. And this foal was sired by old Paint Bucket."

"No question," Ed agreed. "So ... I guess that means the mare's been out in the wild for a year."

"Give or take."

The foal struggled to its feet, and Jake knelt in the straw beside it. "You're a sweet one," he crooned, stroking the soft fur on its withers. He glanced up at Ed. "Of course, you know what this means."

Ed raised his eyebrows, trying to follow Jake's train of thought. "What?"

"We're still short a stallion for this breeding operation."

"Maybe we should let it rest over the winter," Laura said, with a little frown settling between her eyebrows.

"Well, I don't know." Jake stood and came out of the stall. "I'd sure like to know I'm ready in the spring."

He had spent the most of the last year improving his ranch, repairing and enlarging his barn, putting a new roof on the snug house his father built, and making sure he and Laura had plenty of hay, wood, and food stored for the winter. They'd gotten through the first year of marriage with hard work and a loving partnership, but now Jake was ready for more. He wanted to realize his dream of a horse ranch. For that, Ed knew he was right—he needed a stallion. Not just any stallion. Jake wanted the best.

Laura was watching her husband uneasily, and Ed hesitated to voice his thought. He didn't want to upset Laura, but it seemed the only course left to them.

"We could go down Echo Canyon."

"You'd go to the Mormons to trade?" Laura's face paled.

38

"They're not so bad," Ed said.

"You've been into their territory," she said uneasily.

"Yes, as far as Camp Floyd, and Hal has. They're hard workers, and they don't like much to see the Cavalry riding through, but they're pretty much like the rest of us."

"You hear things," Laura said, looking toward Jake.

"I've been over there a little ways once or twice," Jake said. "Don't like what they did a few years back, when Johnston came through, but I reckon it's best to let bygones be bygones and get along."

"Father says that when he came here, Major Buford told him not to trust them."

Jake smiled at her. "It's his job not to trust them, sweetheart, anymore than he can trust the Indians. He's always got to be watching and sending out patrols, and keeping Washington informed of what's going on."

"I could get a week off," Ed said. "Maybe Hal could, too. We could ask the captain to let us scout for remounts."

Jake leaned on the stall door and thought for a moment. "Sure, ask him."

"You're not going without me," Laura said, and Ed looked at her in surprise.

Jake smiled. "Thought you were scared of them."

"Maybe I am, and I don't trust them any more than my father does, but you're not going into Utah without me."

Jake said nothing for several seconds, and Ed waited to see if his brother would let his wife order him around like that.

Laura said softly, urgently, "Jake, you go off for weeks at a time scouting the Indians for Father, and I worry the whole time. I don't think I can sit home and wonder what's happening to you in Utah."

"Thought you got over worrying about me visiting the Indians," Jake said.

"I did. When you took me with you."

"I don't think this expedition is dangerous," Jake said. "It's business."

"Then take me."

She wasn't begging or whining, just making a good argument. Ed didn't know if he would be able to refuse such a request from a beautiful, intelligent woman, especially if he knew that she loved him. He listened with avid interest. Would Jake see it as a challenge to his authority in the family?

Jake drew a deep breath and looked at his brother. "Laura and I will ride up to the fort tomorrow and see what the captain thinks."

Ed exhaled. He wasn't going to get to hear the end of this discussion, he could see that.

"I'd best get back to the fort now, but I'll tell Hal."

"Do that," said Jake. "And tell him it's a girl."

Chapter 9

Iris stalled as long as she could over the dishpan. Betsy and Catherine were drying the dishes, and they were far too efficient. Iris moved slower and slower.

"Come on," Catherine said at last. "I want to get done. You're pokey tonight."

Betsy tossed her head. "Leave her alone."

"Father said we can take our quilt squares outside after chores, but it's going to be dark by the time we're done."

Betsy grabbed the linen towel her sister was holding. "Go on, then. I'll finish."

Catherine's eyes grew wide. "Really?"

"Yes. Just go."

Catherine looked at Iris. "Do you mind?"

"No, it's all right." Iris kept her head bent studiously over the kettle she was scrubbing.

Without another word, Catherine dashed up the stairs. She came back down with her work bag and ran out the back door.

Iris and Betsy worked in silence, but at last Iris couldn't delay giving her the last pan to dry.

"Did you wipe the table?" Betsy asked softly.

"Y—well, perhaps not thoroughly." Iris squeezed out the dishrag and went back to the long plank table. It was clean, and Betsy knew it was clean, but Iris ran the cloth back and forth over the surface again and again, wondering just how long she could delay her entrance to the parlor.

"You're keeping Rufus waiting." Eleanor spoke from the doorway. Her expression was cold and displeased.

"I—yes, ma'am." Iris turned away and hung up the dishcloth, then slowly untied her apron strings. Betsy's stricken look was no consolation. Iris glanced toward the doorway. Eleanor was waiting to be sure she fulfilled her duty.

Iris followed her to the parlor door, staring down at her worn black shoes. Eleanor stepped aside. "Rufus, here's Iris to sit with you." She gave Iris's arm a little pull, and Iris stepped into the room.

"Sit down," said Eleanor.

Iris raised her chin. Rufus was sitting straight as a poker on the edge of the settee. It was a rough wooden seat, no doubt made by his father, with thin corduroy cushions. Rufus clasped his hands together between his knees and looked up at her, smiling his vacant smile.

Iris edged toward a straight chair. She heard the door close behind her and flinched.

"Sit," said Rufus.

She perched on the edge of the chair.

"Naw, over here."

She swallowed and shook her head. "We're supposed to talk. Get acquainted."

"Says who?"

"It's the custom." She looked desperately toward the door, but there was no hope of a chaperone joining them.

"You want to talk?" he asked with a puzzled air.

"Of course." She realized she was trembling and laced her fingers together.

"What about?"

Iris looked around the small room. "It's a nice parlor."

He shrugged.

"Who's the woman in that picture?" She gestured toward a miniature painting that sat on a side table next to Brother Zale's book that held the prophet's words. Its frame was a thick wooden oval.

"My ma."

She nodded, but she could see little likeness to careworn Eleanor. "She was very pretty then."

42

"It was when she was in Illinois. Her pa was rich, and he had her picture made. Long time ago."

It was the most Iris had ever heard him say at one time. Perhaps Rufus could be humanized after all.

He frowned suddenly. "Come over here. You're supposed to set with me."

Iris said quickly, "So, your folks came from Illinois? My family was in Missouri before we came here. My father was born in Connecticut, though."

"Look, we're getting married," Rufus said, louder this time.

"I—yes."

"Don't you like me?"

The sick feeling was making Iris's stomach roil, and she couldn't answer.

He stood up and grabbed her wrist. "You have to like me, you know." He pulled her to her feet and toward him, but Iris leaned back, resisting his force.

"Don't! Leave me alone!"

"What's the matter?"

He jerked her toward him and tried to grasp her shoulder with his other hand, but Iris reached quickly toward the little cherry table. Her hand closed around the heavy picture frame.

"Let me go!"

"Not yet." His fingers dug into her forearm. "You need to learn some courtin' manners."

As he pulled her roughly toward him, she brought her arm up as fast and hard as she could, aiming for his skull. He twisted at the last second, a fleeting look of shock in his eyes, and the edge of the frame connected with his cheekbone.

He yelped and leaped away from her. Iris stood for only an instant, staring in horror at the broken frame. She set it hastily on the table and ran for the door.

"Hey! Get back here!"

"No!"

43

"We're getting married!"

Iris opened the door. "Not for ten days," she gasped. "And, no, I don't like you!" She slammed the door and ran up the stairs weeping.

~~~~~

When Rufus came in from milking the next morning, he was subdued. He slunk in after his father and Luke, sitting at the end of the table farthest from the stove where Iris was frying the bacon.

Eleanor and Betsy were helping get breakfast on, and they shuttled back and forth from the stove to the table with coffee, porridge, fried potatoes, eggs and bacon. Iris kept her back to the men. Although it was very hot so close to the cook stove, she didn't want to get any closer to Rufus or Isaac. Delia and Catherine came in with Delia's three little ones and settled in around the table.

"What in tarnation happened to you?" Betsy's voice was loud, and everyone turned to look at her, where she stood holding the platter of eggs. She was staring at Rufus, and the collective gaze shifted to him.

Iris caught her breath as she saw the purple bruise that darkened the right side of his face. *I didn't do that,* she wanted to scream. Then she noticed a smaller, mottled blotch surrounding an inch-long gash below his left eye.

"Hush," said Isaac, and Iris dared to look his way. He was sipping his coffee as though nothing was wrong.

"But he—"

"I said hush," Isaac barked, and Betsy's head drooped. She slid two eggs onto Rufus's plate.

He grunted and picked up his fork, wincing as he brought his arm up.

Iris turned away quickly, before he could catch her staring.

After everyone had eaten and the men went out to their work again, Iris, Catherine, and Eleanor put the kitchen to rights. At last the dishes were done once more, and Betsy came breezing to the kitchen carrying her egg basket.

"Iris, come help me pick eggs."

"You don't need help for that," her mother said.

"I think one of the hens is hiding a nest," Betsy replied.

"Well, be quick. I need you girls to help me pickle all that cabbage today."

"We will be."

Betsy dashed for the door, and Iris hurried after her without looking toward Eleanor. When they reached the chicken coop, Betsy turned, breathless.

"While you were doing dishes, I found out what happened to Rufus."

"How did you do that?"

"Delia told me. She'll tell me anything that makes my ma's children look bad."

Iris frowned. She hadn't ought to listen, but her curiosity got the better of her. "So?"

"Ma told Pa last night that you was crying, and that you broke her portrait on Rufus's thick head because he tried to kiss you. Pa took Rufus out to the woodshed and give him a licking."

"Wh—" It was incredible. Iris just stared for a moment, then shook her head. "You mean your father stuck up for me? He punished Rufus for trying to assault me?"

Betsy blinked. "That's not what Delia said. Not at all."

"What did she say?"

"She said Pa yelled at Rufus and told him he was an idiot to let you push him around. He said Rufus better learn to keep his woman in line. Then he pounded him a couple of times and told him to grow up and be a man."

Iris felt weak. She reached out and grabbed a post that held up a row of nesting boxes.

"I—I have to go back and help your mother."

Betsy nodded, her eyes huge. "Iris, I don't want you to marry Rufus. Not if you don't want to."

"I don't," she whispered.

45

Betsy nodded. "I think you're fine the way you are. I don't think you're an insolent, domineering shrew."

"Who said that?"

"You don't want to know."

"I do if it was my future husband."

"No, it was Delia. But you probably shouldn't have hit him."

"I had to."

"But Ma's picture!"

Iris sighed. "That was unfortunate. Is it ruined?"

"I don't know. Iris, what are we going to do?"

"We?" Iris said with a tiny laugh.

"Yes. I feel like—like you're—" Betsy gulped a sob. "Like you're my sister now. I hate to say it, but Ma and Delia won't be any help to you. And I just feel like whatever happens to you can happen to me. You know?"

Iris reached for Betsy's hand and squeezed it. "Yes. Yes, I know."

Chapter 10

Ed Sherman slouched in the saddle, letting his mind wander as he followed his brother and sister-in-law along the dusty trail. He was riding Jake's dun, Tramp, again. They'd been out for over a week, scouring the countryside for decent horses, and he was getting trail weary.

It had been a good week, all in all, though the nights were cold. Ed felt closer to his brother than he had in years, and he'd gotten to know Jake's wife better. He'd stood in awe of Laura at first. Not only was she an undisputed beauty with golden hair and vibrant blue eyes, she was also the daughter of Ed's commanding officer, Captain Andrew Byington, whom everyone liked and respected.

But somehow, spending a week in the Utah wilderness, drinking coffee from the same dented coffee pot, and watching her take her turns caring for the horses they purchased had made her seem more accessible. She was still far above the common run of pioneer women he met in his duties at Fort Bridger, and he could still scarcely believe his quiet brother had snagged her, but he could admit now that she was human. An extraordinary human, but unpretentious and companionable, even though to Ed she still seemed incomparable.

He didn't like foraying so deeply into Mormon territory, but if Jake was going to establish his horse herd quickly, he had to get some topnotch breeding stock. The animals that came limping into Fort Bridger after months on the rugged trail with wagon trains wouldn't do.

The bay mare they had captured in the mountains was a good start, but Jake's other hoses—his working mounts—were steady, dependable geldings. They'd given up on the paint stallion, and Jake didn't think the other mustang mares in the hills near the family's homestead were good investments of his time. So here they were.

The Mormons were an enigma to Ed. His fellow soldiers had a decided dislike for them, and some of that had rubbed off on him.

Three years ago General Johnston had expected to ride down Echo Canyon and bring Utah to its knees in one swoop. It hadn't happened. The army's disdain for the Mormons had turned to annoyance, then hatred. The "saints" had kept them busy, attacking the wagon trains that were Johnston's vital supply source. They'd reached a truce, but the federal government had compromised more than Ed thought was prudent, and while the army was now free to patrol the Utah territory, their power was woefully restricted. If the military pressed its authority too far, there would be regrets all around.

Ed was uncomfortable riding out here without a solid military detachment behind him, which was the usual way the dragoons traveled out here when they patrolled. His brother was a civilian and seemed able to live at peace with everyone in the Wyoming territory—Indians, settlers and soldiers alike. But this side of the boundary it was different. The Mormons weren't as ready to accept Jake, weren't willing to trust him immediately. They'd met a few ranchers who were friendly and willing to trade, but most coldly sent them on their way.

Laura held Spook back until Ed's horse came up beside her. "I'm glad you came with us."

"Me, too, but I'm glad we're leaving this wasteland soon."

Laura smiled. "We've certainly got better terrain in Wyoming. But they've done well out here."

Ed looked around at the barren, rocky landscape. "Don't see how they can grow a thing. They wear their people out. Use them up and go recruit more. They're bringing young people over from Europe, you know."

"I heard that. Father told me about the bunch that came through pulling handcarts." Laura shrugged. "If you believe in something strongly enough..."

Ed shook his head. "They have no idea what they're getting into when they join up."

"Well, it's not a society I'd choose," Laura admitted. "Still, their horses are the best I've seen in months. They're keeping them fit somehow."

Ed had to admit it was true. During their dozen years in Utah, the Mormons had managed to coax the desert to produce, and the four sleek mares Jake had bought for his herd were the proof. Ed's part in the expedition was to pick up any sound remounts he could for the cavalry troops stationed at Fort Bridger, where Captain Byington was in command, but the prices the Mormons asked were higher than the army could afford. It was all right for Jake and his fancy breeding stock, but the money the captain had entrusted to Ed would only stretch so far. He'd bought a big, well-mannered gelding for the captain, but that was Byington's own money, not the army's.

Jake's search for the ideal stallion had been disappointing. He had been almost ready to turn homeward with the horses they had acquired when they'd heard of a rancher who had a superior colt. Laura had readily agreed to extend the trip, but Ed was getting restless. He ought to get back to the fort soon. When they set out for Zale's ranch, they left the horses they had already purchased with a farmer at the base of Echo Canyon, near the trail back to Fort Bridger. They had ridden half the day to get this far.

Jake halted his horse and waited for them to catch up. "Down there."

Ed stretched to see down into the valley before them. Smoke curled up from a chimney, and a neat homestead was laid out before them. One paddock held a cluster of sheep, round with their full crop of wool as November drew close. The chilly nights promised cold weather soon, and the ewes would be snug against the snow Ed knew would soon immobilize the valley.

A large pasture stretched beside the trail, and far down near the farm buildings several horses were grazing in corrals.

As they approached the ranch house, Ed almost wished the trip wasn't coming to a close. It had been rough, going from farm to farm, looking for the perfect horse, and Jake especially had been disappointed that Hal was not with them. Ed would have appreciated Hal's presence, too, but their friend had drawn another assignment, riding up toward the Sweetwater to bring in a late supply convoy.

"If Zale doesn't have what you want, we'll have to turn back, Jake," Edward said.

"I know." Jake looked over the corrals hopefully. "I hate to come all this way and go home empty-handed."

"I still think we can catch that paint," Ed said eagerly. "I know he's not perfect, but he and the mares you bought this week would make a nice little herd to start with."

"No, he's no good." Jake squinted against the westering sun. "He's feisty, but he's still ugly as sin. Besides, that paint's got to be getting old."

Laura smiled across at her brother-in-law. "Someday people will come from all over the territory to buy fine horses from the Sherman ranch."

Ed's head snapped up as a shrill whinny rang out. He pulled Tramp to a halt, and Jake and Laura's horses stopped, too. Across the valley floor, a red horse sped toward them the length of the vast pasture. He held his head high as he galloped proudly, his mane streaming behind him.

Slowly Jake smiled. "Now that's a horse."

"You think that's the one?" Ed asked.

"I don't know. I hope so."

The magnificent stallion loped along inside the fence as they rode on toward the house. He kept pace for a few strides, then pulled away to tear out into the pasture, but always he returned to watch them, snorting as he paced along inside the enclosure. Spook whinnied, but Laura slapped his neck.

50

"Hush, you. He's just showing off."

Even Shakespeare and Tramp pranced a little as the red stallion huffed and pawed. The late sun gleamed on his flanks, casting a bright luster on his reddish coat. His mane and tail were the same vivid hue, and his face was sweet and sensitive. He was young, Ed judged, probably four or five years old, but only a good look at his teeth would tell for sure.

"He's perfect," Laura breathed, and Jake's smile deepened. His gaze lingered on the stallion's long legs, deep chest and rounded quarters as he walked Shakespeare slowly onward.

Ed exhaled slowly. "I see what you mean. He makes that mustang look second rate."

Even steady Tramp seemed little more than a plug next to the bright chestnut stallion, but at least Ed wasn't riding a mule. Hal had tried to get him a horse from the fort's string, but his sergeant had refused permission. So Ed had borrowed Tramp again and put up with the dun's rough trot for a week. He wished he had his own horse. Maybe he could work something out with Jake after they got home.

As they approached the plain but solid ranch house, several children tore across the yard to the door, and a black and buff dog appeared near the barn, barking. A woman with wispy gray hair came to the doorway, wiping her hands on her apron.

"Hush, you," she scolded the dog. "Luke, tie him up."

A half-grown boy slipped past her and ambled toward the dog. "Shut up," he snarled, kicking at the dog. It cowered, and the boy dragged it into the barn.

Jake rode Shakespeare up close to the doorstep and tipped his hat. "Ma'am. We're looking for the Zale ranch."

"This be the place."

"My name is Jake Sherman, and I'm hoping to buy a horse. Is your husband at home?"

The woman looked him over slowly, then turned her scrutiny on Ed. When she looked at Laura, her eyes crinkled up in a squint. Ed could almost hear her brain trying to categorize the beautiful girl who sat so easily on the huge gray horse.

"This be your wife?" the woman asked at last.

"Yes, ma'am." Jake's smile was gentle.

"How far have you rid?"

"From Fort Bridger."

Her pale eyebrows twitched. "'Light and water your horses. I'll send one of the young'uns for their pa."

Ed swung gratefully from the saddle and led Tramp toward the wooden trough in the dooryard. Next to it, the well had been topped with a round stone berm. He lowered the wooden bucket into the well. Jake dismounted and went to Spook's side to give Laura a hand. The colorless woman disappeared inside the house, and a few seconds later they heard a door bang shut at the back of the structure. Ed dropped Tramp's reins and sauntered to the paddock fence at the side of the house, and he could see the boy, Luke, running barefoot, deeper down valley.

When he turned back to the well, Jake was watering Spook and Shakespeare, and Laura stood stretching prettily. Her golden braid hung down her back, from beneath the soft felt hat she habitually wore. Her split skirt and pale blue shirtwaist still looked becoming, although she'd been camping in primitive conditions for a week. Ed couldn't understand how a woman could do that without a baggage train, but Laura seemed to have mastered the art of travel.

A second woman came from the house, carrying a basket. She was much younger than the first, and her brown hair was pulled severely back in a twist. Her homespun dress was a cheerful burgundy tone, but functional in design.

"Eleanor says you've come a far piece. We thought you'd like some refreshment." She held the basket out to Laura.

"Why, thank you." Laura hesitated, then said, "Would you be Mrs. Zale?"

The woman laughed mirthlessly. "Oh, yes, I most certainly would be."

"I'm Laura Sherman."

Her brilliant smile was too sincere to ignore, and the other woman succumbed. Her lips curved slowly, reluctantly. "I'm Delia."

"It's nice to meet you ladies, after so many days on the trail with my husband and his brother." Laura spoke quietly, but graciously, and Mrs. Zale was plainly won over.

She flushed slightly and looked toward the house. "Brother Zale doesn't like us to have strangers in, especially gentiles, but you're welcome to sit in the shade over there. There's gingerbread here, and the well water is good."

"Thank you, that's most kind." Laura smiled encouragingly at Jake, and he removed his hat.

"Thank you, ma'am."

Ed nodded. "Ma'am." Tramp lifted his nose from the watering trough and sprayed drops of water all over him. When Ed had caught the reins and led him a few feet away, Delia was gone.

"Guess we wait for Brother Zale," he muttered.

"Could be worse," Laura said complacently.

She never complained, Ed realized. That one time she'd declared she wouldn't sit home worrying about her husband was the closest he'd heard her come to it. Did Jake know what a jewel he had found? No matter where her husband took her, Laura was content just to be near him and be part of his adventures. Yes, Ed decided, Jake knew. The way his brother's eyes followed her told him Jake's estimate of her worth. Bringing Laura on the trip hadn't been a show of weakness. Instead, it showed the strength of his faith in her, in her ability to be a good traveler and a help along the trail. Ed hoped he would be so blessed one day.

"Go sit in the shade, sweetheart," Jake said. "We'll tie these critters up. There's a little grass over there by the fence row."

"I think I'll explore." Laura smiled impudently. "Think Brother Zale will mind?"

She was looking off to one side of the house, toward a small outbuilding between it and the barn. Ed thought he caught a flash of color as he glanced toward it.

"Just don't get lost." Jake pulled a length of rope from his saddle and slipped Shakespeare's bridle off over his ears.

"It'll be cold tonight," Ed said.

Jake nodded. "We've got three or four hours of daylight left. If we can get back up to the Glucks' ranch, we'll be home tomorrow night."

"That would good." Ed tied Tramp to a fencepost and sat down, leaning back in the dried weeds. The day was warm for the season, but he knew the temperature could drop below freezing within hours. "I'll be glad when we're back over the line."

"What line?"

"You know, the line that separates the territory where we're good, upstanding citizens from the one where we're suspicious gentiles."

Jake settled down near him and pulled his hat low over his eyes.

Chapter 11

Laura walked briskly along the side of the pole barn and stooped to enter the chicken coop. The girl she had seen flit inside was close to her age, she thought, and she was starved for the companionship of a young woman. She heard a gasp and stood still, letting her eyes adjust to the dimness.

"I'm sorry. I didn't mean to startle you." She took off her hat and wiped her forehead on the sleeve of her cotton blouse. "I'm Laura Sherman."

"Is your husband the man on the bay horse?"

"Yes. He's hoping to buy a colt from your father."

There was an instant's silence, and then the girl said softly, "He's not my father."

Laura's heart sank. She had refused to think it might be possible. "Surely he's not your husband."

"No. I'm betrothed to Brother Zale's son." The girl turned away from her and stooped to feel inside one of the nest boxes lined up on the wall inside the little shed.

"Is the wedding soon?" The girl seemed reticent, and Laura spoke cheerfully. She wasn't used to being rebuffed. The long pause made her wonder if the girl hadn't heard her.

"Yes," she said at last. "It's—well, they put it off once, but it's soon."

"Ah. So, Delia will be your mother-in-law? She seems so young!"

"She is young. Look, I shouldn't be speaking with you. But Rufus is not her son. He's Eleanor's."

"But ... I thought ..." Laura swallowed.

"You saw two women out there."

"Yes. One of them, Delia, said she was Mrs. Zale."

"She's a sister wife."

"Sister ... you mean—?" Laura felt suddenly stupid and unsophisticated.

The girl faced her again, her lips tightening in a bitter smile. "It's the custom here."

In the poor light, Laura saw hopelessness in the girl's face. Her breathing was rapid and uneven. Something was definitely wrong.

"I'm sorry. I didn't mean to pry. It's just that I don't meet many women where we live, and—"

She broke off as the girl brushed a tear from her lashes. She was striking, Laura thought, though her hair was hidden beneath a calico bonnet and her skin was tanned. She had a clear complexion and introspective dark eyes that glittered with sorrow. She was younger than Laura had supposed, and she had a fragility about her, but at the same time radiated a toughness Laura respected.

She dared to ask, "This man you're marrying, how old is he?"

"Nineteen. The same as me."

Laura frowned. "You don't seem happy. Is this your choice?" she asked softly.

The girl looked anxiously past her, toward the doorway. She dropped her voice to a near whisper. "No, it's not my choice."

Laura wasn't sure if there was an apt response to that declaration. She felt sheltered and naive. "I'm sorry to seem so dense, but ... I was hoping Eleanor was Delia's mother-in-law. Forgive me. I've been unspeakably rude."

The girl shrugged. "It's not your fault. I expect you come from a place where this seems very strange."

"But surely you can refuse to marry a man you don't love?"

"Please, they don't like us to talk to gentiles."

"I'm sorry. I don't want to cause trouble for you. Do you want me to leave?"

The girl worked in silence for a moment, shoving her hand under a roosting hen and pulling out a tan egg. Then she turned her face fully toward Laura in frank curiosity. "Were you allowed to choose your own husband?"

"Yes. And I picked the best man in Wyoming."

The look that crossed her features was indefinable. Laura wondered if the young woman thought she was lying, or if she believed Laura had truly been given the freedom to decide her own fate.

The girl turned abruptly to the next nesting box. "How can you be certain he will never want another woman?"

Laura felt indignation rising within her. "Jake would never, ever think such a thing."

The girl nodded soberly. "You should be very thankful."

Laura stood staring at her for a moment, her heart full of pity for this young woman and gratitude for God's outpouring of grace to her. This girl's family had chosen one path, her own another. How easily she might have been in this situation.

"I am thankful." She reached out and touched the girl's shoulder. "What is your name?"

"Iris."

Laura smiled. "A lovely flower."

"One that loves water," Iris said with regret. "Something we don't see enough of in these parts."

"We saw irrigation ditches as we came down the valley."

"Yes, they're very industrious. Make a crop at any cost."

"How long have you been here with the Zales?"

"Over two months now. I was supposed to be married after harvest, but Brother Zale had second thoughts as to whether I would fit in with his family."

Laura wondered what that meant. Had the boy's father, who already was in her mind a monster, wanted to test Iris somehow, to see if she could work hard enough, or had he wanted to see if his son's initial attraction to her would last?

"And then we had a bad windstorm," Iris said, "and the new addition fell in, and the cattle stampeded. It took the men a week to find all the steers and bring them home. After that it was weeks before they were finished building and repairing the damage to the roof. But now they say it's time, and I must wed Rufus Zale next week."

"And your parents approve of this plan?"

"My mother is dead, and my father's been gone a long time." Iris slid her hand beneath a setting hen and plucked an egg from the straw.

"But who has been taking care of you?"

Iris continued her hunt as she spoke in a low tone. "I was to marry another young man two years ago." Her eyes flicked to Laura's and away. "My father was here then, and I had some say in the matter."

"You loved him? The man you were to marry then?"

Iris shrugged. "I only met him twice. I thought he was a nice boy. As nice as anyone, and …" She stopped, and her long, dark lashes swept downward. "I would have been the first wife. The only, I hoped."

"What happened?"

Her lips tightened. "Frank drowned. His wagon went through the ice on the river. I was allowed to grieve for a time, but then my father was assigned to lead an expedition looking for minerals. I couldn't go with him, and I was placed with an elder's family. I'm older than the usual age for marriage in these parts now, and … well, the elders decided it was time I became a wife. But the man they've chosen for me—oh, it's hard."

"Are you frightened?"

Iris sobbed. "Please. It's best if you—"

Laura stepped toward her. "Iris, God ordained marriage between a man and a woman. I believe the kind of marriage Jake and I have is the type described in the Scripture. Do you have a Bible?"

She shook her head. "They have writings. Brother Zale reads from the prophet's words."

58

Laura noted that Iris distanced herself from the church with her words. "I have a small Bible portion that I carry with me. My father gave it to me. It's only the New Testament, but it speaks much of Christ, and it also mentions marriage." She reached into the deep pocket of her riding skirt and pulled out the tiny, leather-bound book. She had treasured it, but she knew that eventually she could replace it. Iris might never have another chance to lay hands on a Bible.

"I can't take it."

"You must. Read it for yourself, Iris. It is God's own words. Read the books of Ephesians and Titus. The apostle Paul had much to say to women."

The girl's hand trembled as she slowly tucked the book into her basket. Laura hoped her gift would not bring trouble down on Iris, and that she would have time to read it before she was bound to Rufus Zale irrevocably.

A shadow darkened the room, and Iris looked swiftly toward the doorway. Laura started, feeling a sudden dread, but it was Edward who stood blinking in the dimness.

"Laura? Jake has struck his bargain with Mr. Zale."

"He's bought the chestnut?" A thrill coursed through her at Jake's success.

"No, Zale wouldn't sell him, but he had another stallion in the barn, the sire of the one you saw. We're almost ready to leave."

Laura saw that Edward's eyes had adjusted to the twilight in the hen house, and his gaze was now fixed on Iris. The girl stood immobile, staring down at the straw-strewn floor, seemingly trying to hide.

"Ed, this is Iris ... I'm sorry, I didn't get your last name." Laura smiled at her new friend.

Iris's reply was nearly inaudible. "Perkins."

"Not Zale?" Edward was smiling with the same gentle but probing look his brother often wore.

Iris turned slightly away from him, shifting her egg basket to her other arm. "No, it's Perkins. I am a guest here for the next week."

Ed seemed puzzled by her listlessness. He glanced at Laura, and she saw a flicker of concern in his wide brown pupils.

"Iris, this is my husband's brother, Edward Sherman." Laura deliberately put a light, cheerful note in her voice.

"I must go in," Iris murmured, but she didn't move toward the doorway, where Edward still stood.

"Walk with me." Laura touched her sleeve gently, but Iris pulled away.

"No, I mustn't. Brother Zale would be angry."

Edward's eyes widened in question, but Laura didn't respond. She could explain to him later, but now she knew she had only moments to get through to Iris.

"Is there anything I can do?"

"No. Just go. Do not say that we have spoken, please, Mrs. Sherman."

Laura hesitated. "All right, but surely you can do something to change this unhappy circumstance. There are always choices, Iris."

"Is there a problem?" Ed asked, his eyes lingering on Iris.

The girl looked at him briefly, then at Laura, and Laura saw no hope in her eyes.

"I've not heard from my father and brother in six months. They may be deceased. I have no protector now, Mrs. Sherman. I thought when the wind storm came that perhaps God had sent it to spare me from the wedding. But that is past, and now I am told I will stand before the bishop with Rufus next week. You tell me … what choice do I have?"

Laura stood helpless, unable to answer.

Come with us, she wanted to say, but she didn't dare. The girl had made it plain that interference would not be welcome. What trouble would she bring on Jake if she urged this young woman to defy the Mormon leaders?

She stepped closer to Iris. "We live close to Fort Bridger. Everyone in the area knows my husband, and my father is the commanding officer at the fort. If you ever need a friend outside Utah …"

Iris pulled away with a little sob. "Please. Brother Zale will be very angry if he knows I spoke to you. Just tell your husband—" She broke off, looking wildly from Laura to Ed.

"What is it?"

Iris took several shallow breaths. "Nothing. It's just … Brother Zale sets great store by that stallion. Your husband must have paid a high price."

"Zale is keeping the colt," Ed said uncertainly.

Iris nodded. "Yes, well, be careful."

Laura looked at Ed, but he was clearly as baffled as she was. She squeezed Iris's shoulder gently. "Good-bye, friend. Don't despair." She turned and went out into the bright sunlight, and Ed followed. He said nothing as they walked past the barn toward the corral, where Jake was deep in conversation with a burly, gray-bearded man. A younger man with red hair and a muscular frame stood beside him, and he turned to watch Ed and Laura as they approached. *The dreaded Rufus, no doubt,* Laura thought.

Their horses were ready for travel, and a proud sorrel stallion was cross-tied between Shakespeare and Tramp. He resembled the other stallion, with the same impressive carriage, but his mane and tail were pale against his red hide. He snorted and high-stepped, sidling away from first one gelding, then the other. The younger chestnut stallion ran back and forth in his enclosure, whinnying and stomping. Laura hoped they could get the sorrel away without any trouble from the other horses.

One glance at Mr. Zale was enough. His full beard did not hide his bold leer. Laura pulled her hat on and took Spook's reins. She led him several steps away before she mounted, putting the horse's body between her and the men. When she swung up into the saddle, she could feel the sharp eyes raking over her. She didn't look at the men again, and cringed when he said loudly, "So that's the missus?"

She turned Spook toward the trail and walked him a few paces, losing Jake's reply. She waited at the gate to the yard, feeling very exposed. Her skin crawled, and she longed suddenly for a bath. *This is how Iris feels,* she thought. *Except Iris has no escape.*

She looked toward the house behind the men. Above their heads, two children were peeking from behind a curtain at an upstairs window. Laura looked at the other windows, and saw a flutter at one. Yes, it was Iris, she was sure. She made no sign, except to lift her chin and smile briefly.

Jake and Ed didn't come immediately, as she had expected. She waited, stroking Spook's neck. Jake was speaking earnestly to Zale, and the older man seemed to be disagreeing. The son was just listening, his slack mouth hanging open.

Lord, please do something to help Iris, Laura prayed silently. *Don't leave her in this awful situation.*

Isaac Zale's voice rose. "A handshake is enough out here. This ain't St. Louis."

She strained to hear Jake's answer. "Well, sir, my brother's right. I'm not of your persuasion, and folks don't know me well around here. I'm taking this horse out of the Utah territory. Someone might question my ownership."

Laura held her breath. Instinct told her that Jake would not do himself any favors by intimating distrust of Isaac Zale. Their conversation continued, and at last Zale and his son walked into the house. She urged Spook closer to Jake and Ed.

"What's happening?" she whispered.

"He's getting me a bill of sale."

"He didn't want to."

Jake shrugged. His brown eyes narrowed with concern as he looked toward the house. "Some men, you just get a feeling. I like the horse, but from what I see and what Ed told me..."

"What do you think she meant, when she said *be careful?*" Ed asked her.

"I don't know. I suppose she might mean the horse can be dangerous."

Jake eyed the stallion doubtfully. "I can handle him."

Ed gave a tug at Tramp's girth. "I wondered if she was hinting we might be raided on the trail. They say some of these fellows have tame Indians they use to get what they—" He stopped suddenly, and Laura knew Zale was coming back. She moved Spook to the far side of Ed's mount, without looking toward him.

"I thank you, sir," Jake said heartily. "Nice doing business with you."

Chapter 12

They rode up the valley with Jake leading the stallion. The horse pulled at the lead line constantly and snapped at the other horses, which they all found annoying.

"I hope we can make it back to the Glucks' place, and not camp on the trail tonight," Ed said. The sun was sinking toward the western plain, and the breeze had turned chilly.

"Got to," Jake said.

Laura nodded. "Yes, we can't camp out with that animal to keep track of. We wouldn't get any sleep."

Ed felt easier knowing they were all agreed. There were too many unknowns, and he wanted to be where the animals would be secure during the darkness. No doubt Jake felt the same way.

"Wait up." They were out of sight of Zale's house, and Jake halted Shakespeare and dismounted.

"What are you doing?" Ed asked.

"This horse is so ornery, I'm going to put the saddle on him. Maybe work some of the kinks out of him."

"Zale had him tied up in the barn," Ed said, reaching for Shakespeare's reins. "Why do you suppose that was?"

Jake shrugged. "One stud's enough in the pasture."

"Does he have a name?" Laura sat on her big gray, watching as Jake switched his gear to the sorrel.

"Zale said he called him Red, but I don't go for that."

"We'll think of a suitable name," Laura said.

"I'll lead Shakespeare for you." Ed slipped the lead line over Shakespeare's head. Jake's sanguine gelding was content to jog along behind Tramp.

The moment Jake landed in the saddle, the stallion began to paw and lunge.

"We should have brought a different bridle." Ed ruefully eyed the light snaffle Jake had transferred from Shakespeare. Jake liked to use the most gentle bit he could on a horse, but sometimes a curb was indicated.

"He wants to run, all right," Jake said between his teeth. "Keep your horses in, and I'll give him a little exercise."

He turned the sorrel up the trail and gave him some slack in the reins. The stallion took off flying, beating the earth with his hooves and snorting with each fling of his regal head.

Ed shook his head. "He's working himself twice as hard as he has to."

The red horse seemed to love throwing himself about. When Jake circled him back toward them, the stallion kept up his frantic pace, and reluctantly slowed when Jake applied strong pressure to the bit and leaned back to shift the center of his weight to the horse's hindquarters.

"He's a race horse," Ed called when Jake came within earshot, and Jake laughed.

"He might give Spook a run for his money."

"Well, I don't feel like racing," Laura warned him. "Ugh! Keep him away."

The sorrel nipped sharply at Spook's withers in passing, and his teeth came close to Laura's knee.

"You two come along at your own pace. I'll wear him down a little," Jake called, heading off up the trail once more. The sorrel got his head down and bolted.

Ed was beginning to wonder if they'd made a big mistake. Was the horse always this full of energy, or was he just tired of confinement and eager to stretch his legs? And what had the mysterious girl meant when she'd told him and Laura to warn Jake to be careful?

Chapter 13

Iris kept busy until twilight, helping Elmer and Luke clean out the barn. It was hard, messy work, but she welcomed it because she knew Eleanor and Delia wouldn't venture out here unless Brother Zale demanded it, and he and Rufus had gone back to the far pasture to work on the irrigation ditches until dark. She hoped they would come home so late and tired that she could for one more evening escape the terrifying ritual of parlor sitting with Rufus.

She had gone through it once since the night she clobbered him with the miniature, under duress, and she was determined not to go through it again. She had refused that other time until Delia had stepped forward and volunteered to chaperone. Rufus was angry, but Delia had pulled her husband aside and somehow convinced him that it would do no harm to initiate Iris to the courting procedure gradually.

She had sat rigid beside Rufus for twenty-nine minutes. Delia had openly scorned Iris's nervousness, but her presence had kept Rufus in line for the most part. Delia had also introduced several topics of conversation, and Iris had seized them gratefully. When Rufus grasped her hand in his hot, sweaty ones, she had writhed a bit and suffered Delia's rebuke for it.

"He's your fiancé, child. You're plenty old enough to accept a man's advances."

When Delia started to rise, saying she would bring tea, Iris said quickly, "No, thank you. I don't care for tea tonight."

Rufus shrugged. "You don't care for anything." He didn't seem to realize that Iris had foiled Delia's attempt to leave them alone.

When the proscribed time was up, Iris leaped up, pulling her
hand from Rufus's. "Good-night," she stammered, and fled upstairs.

Delia seemed to find the awkward wooing amusing, and Iris
could tell she was determined the wedding would go forward.
Perhaps she wanted to insure that the extra worker would not leave
them.

Delia's next baby was due in the spring, though you couldn't tell
yet from looking at her. She'd spilled the news intentionally, Iris
thought, as a sort of one-upmanship to Eleanor. Elmer, at nine, was
the youngest of Eleanor's eight children, but Delia was still in her
prime. She would not let the first wife forget that.

Maybe she also let the news out as advance warning to Iris—she
wouldn't be helping with the heavy work this winter. Guess who
would be doing the laundry, shoveling, and scrubbing? Not Delia.
Her pregnancy would be the perfect excuse to avoid work. Not
Eleanor. Her seniority gave her the privilege of choosing the gentler
chores: cooking, sewing, and spinning. The sons and daughters of the
house would pick up the slack, but Iris was already pressed into
service in the most arduous tasks.

She didn't mind earning her keep. In fact, the thought had
crossed her mind many times that she could offer to stay on as a
hired girl. She would give the Zales good measure in return for her
keep this winter so long as they allowed her to remain single and
share the little room under the eaves with Betsy and Catherine.

But, no, she knew that was not an option. Delia and Eleanor
might welcome her as a hired girl, but Brother Zale wanted to see his
son married.

When the stalls were clean, Iris sent the boys to carry wood and
water to the kitchen while she stayed in the dim barn to shake out
straw on the floor for bedding. A few animals were kept inside at
night. The rest were left out to pasture, with two ferocious dogs
patrolling.

When her immediate work was done, a ray of light still shone
down onto the valley floor. Iris slipped out the barn door and around

to the west side. She looked all around, then very carefully removed a small black book from her skirt pocket.

Inside the front cover, in a bold hand, was written, "To Laura Byington, from your doting Father. Press on, toward the mark."

She pondered the inscription. What did it mean? It seemed like a word of encouragement. Press on.

Her father was a soldier, golden-haired Laura had told her that. He must have given her this book before her marriage. Iris leafed through the pages. She remembered, long ago, before her family came to this desolate place, that her father had read aloud from a Bible in the evening. Matthew, Mark, Luke, John. Yes, the names were familiar. Her teacher so long ago, back in Missouri, had taught the class to say the books of the Bible by rote. She had even learned some psalms by heart.

Which books had Laura Sherman told her to read? Titus, surely. In the fading light, she caught the title at the top of one of the thin, creamy pages and stopped the flutter of the leaves. A line was drawn along the edge of a passage, and she read it quickly, eager to see what had Laura found profound enough to mark.

"The aged women likewise, that they be in behavior as becometh holiness, not false accusers, not given to much wine, teachers of good things, that they may teach the young women to be sober-minded, to love their husbands, to love their children, to be discreet, chaste, keepers at home, good, obedient to their own husbands, that the word of God be not blasphemed."

Iris read back over the verses so clearly defined by the line of ink. The aged women teaching good things to the young. She supposed it might happen among the Saints, but Eleanor hadn't seemed eager to teach her anything about being a good wife and mother. She'd been warned to be discreet, yes, but loving? It was a distant, almost foreign idea. Her own mother had been loving, but she'd been gone so long. And with her had gone the soft, sweet fragments of her family's former existence.

What about wives being "obedient to their own husbands?" She supposed that meant she was to obey Rufus after next week, just as Eleanor and Delia obeyed Brother Zale. But still, how could Delia consider Isaac her own husband, when he was already someone else's husband? It was confusing.

It was all very well for Laura Sherman to want to love her handsome young man and obey him, but Iris's heart rebelled at even trying to feel those things toward the brutish, dull Rufus. Wasn't there supposed to be some sort of mutual spark between marriage partners? She was certain Laura felt it for her Jake, she'd jumped so quickly to his defense when Iris questioned her.

What if she could never feel that way? Maybe she could have with Frank, but Frank was gone forever. If she couldn't be submissive to Rufus in her heart, would she be blaspheming God, as the Scripture seemed to say?

She shoved the book deep in her pocket with a sigh and turned toward the house. It was too dark to read anymore, and she would go inside and make herself useful. *A keeper at home,* she thought wryly. She would work so hard that no one could ever complain that she didn't carry her weight—*false accusers,* her acute memory taunted.

The sister wives might complain against her, whether she did her share of the work or not. They certainly griped about each other. She'd heard Delia slur Eleanor several times, and she knew Eleanor detested the younger woman her husband had chosen, though she didn't voice it openly. It was obvious to Iris that celestial marriage was a severe trial for both the women.

And she could not picture herself flying to Rufus for comfort and understanding if the others in the house maligned her. Rufus was not the sort of man to comfort a woman in distress. He was more likely to get angry at his wife if others said she was not doing her share of the work.

She had seen the children accused of shirking from time to time, and Brother Zale was not lenient. The boys especially took the brunt of his displeasure. Even Delia had appeared one morning with bruises on her face. It had been a dark, brooding day, and the women had not spoken of it. But when Delia went to change her toddler, Eleanor had hissed, "She doesn't learn."

What was she supposed to learn, Iris wondered. And if no one taught her, would she make the same mistakes Delia did?

The Laura Shermans of this world had loving husbands, doting fathers and even protective brothers-in-law. Edward Sherman's solemn brown eyes were very clear in her mind. *Is there a problem?* he'd asked. What would have happened if she'd said, *Yes, yes, there's a problem. I'm terrified, and I don't want to stay here!* Would his concern and caring for his sister-in-law have extended to include her?

She'd only seen his brother, Laura's beloved Jake, from the window, but she could see that he looked like Edward, and he must have the same character. She tried to stop thinking about the Sherman brothers, but she couldn't. She'd seen Edward's concern, his caution, his deference to Laura. To have a brother like that ... a husband like that.

The comparison to Rufus Zale was too awful. Iris dashed into the kitchen to wash and help get supper on the table.

Chapter 14

It was well after dark when Laura, Jake, and Ed reached the Glucks' farm. The last hour of their journey had been difficult with Jake trying to keep the rambunctious stallion under control and the weary geldings stumbling along in the darkness. Laura hoped they would get a warm reception here. The Glucks had been courteous and friendly on their first meeting, and she was sure they would be again.

"It's late," Philip Gluck said when they arrived. He was young, about Edward's age, with thick brown hair and a neatly trimmed beard. "You'd best stop here overnight."

"Yes, you must," his wife, Mary, insisted. "Put all your horses in the barn, and come eat. I've saved supper, thinking you'd come back tonight, and you'd be hungry."

Laura was surprised at their friendliness. Mary seemed like a regular girl to her, an ordinary young wife. The atmosphere in this home was completely opposite that at the Zales' farm. Apparently not all Mormons avoided giving hospitality to gentiles, she noted.

While the men saw to the livestock, she had a chance to talk to Mary as they put the meal on the table. The Glucks had been married less than a year, and Laura found that she and Mary had much in common. They were both young brides in new homes, learning the ways of the West.

Mary had left her family in New York to join the Mormons. Philip's family had been in the wagon train she came across the plains with, and the Glucks had adopted her, making her feel welcome and accepted. Philip was a generous, amicable young man, and Laura didn't wonder that Mary had fallen in love with him. She only hoped they could sustain their happiness.

"Philip's going to attend a session with the elders at Salt Lake in the spring," Mary said, her eyes shining.

"Is that good?"

"Oh, yes. He's learning more about the church, and they may be thinking of giving him greater responsibility."

Laura wondered if that was something to be excited about. What would Philip learn at the session, and how would it change their world?

She considered mentioning Iris Perkins to Mary, but decided it would not help anyone and could cause friction.

"You've got a nice place, for not having been here long," Laura said.

"Someone else built the house about ten years ago. They moved out last fall." Mary looked away with a frown, and Laura decided it was not polite to mention Johnston's invasion or the unpleasantness that had ensued. They had seen several ruins on their travels, but apparently this house had escaped the destruction. "Philip put the barn up last spring, and lots of Saints came to help. His parents live a couple of hours away, and they came."

"It must be nice to have them so close."

Mary nodded. "I miss my own folks something fierce, but Philip's people have been good to me."

Jake, Ed, and Philip came in from the barn, and Mary poured water into a tin basin for them to wash in.

"We'll put you in our room," Philip said.

"No, don't do that," Laura said quickly.

"We can sleep in the loft," Mary assured her.

"No, Jake and I will be fine in the loft."

Jake looked speculatively to Philip. "Maybe I ought to sleep in the barn."

"No need. I've got dogs I let loose at night."

"Well, the stallion's calmed down some, but he's still pretty restless."

Laura smiled at his understatement. The horse had been so fiery while they traveled that Jake had decided to name him Blaze.

"The horses we left here with you look good," Ed said, "but I can sleep out there if it'll make you feel better, Jake."

Jake stretched, and Laura knew he was taking his time to consider the situation. Her own inclination was to trust Philip Gluck, but Jake was much more experienced in dealing with folks out here. She would keep out of it, although she knew she wouldn't sleep well if Jake were not beside her.

"No, we might as well get a good night's sleep." Jake looked at Philip. "Laura and I will take the loft, though."

Mary smiled. "As you wish, Mr. Sherman. Your brother can sleep down here near the stove if he wishes."

Laura unburdened her heart to Jake in the snug loft that night, repeating in whispers all she could remember of her conversation with Iris Perkins.

"Jake, I hate leaving her there. It's wrong."

He sighed in the darkness. "She's right about one thing. There's nothing we can do. She's part of their world."

"It's not right, Jake." Laura choked and tried to hold back the tears. She knew it would make Jake feel helpless, but she couldn't stop. He held her close, with her head over his heart.

"Let's pray about this."

She squeezed him and listened thankfully while he quietly prayed for Iris, and for a safe journey home with the new horses. Finally she fell into a troubled sleep.

Chapter 15

Ed lay awake for a long time. The floor was hard, but he was warm and dry, and they'd had a good meal. He'd spent a lot of worse nights since he'd joined the Cavalry.

The little farmhouse felt like a home, and Philip and Mary seemed happy. A latent yearning began to stir inside him. Ed wanted a home of his own. The family homestead wasn't his home anymore. It was Jake's and Laura's.

During the first two years of his service in the Cavalry, Ed had been shuffled about, from Fort Laramie to Fort Hall and back, feeling rootless. The wandering life of the dragoons had quickly lost its romance. The drudgery on a military post drove Ed wild. Sometimes in winter he found himself wishing for a foray against hostile Indians, just to relieve the monotony of drill and fatigue details. But his limited experience in battle had soon taught him that keeping peace was the preferable course.

He'd spent three months as a striker for a captain's family, which wasn't so bad. He'd earned a little extra money. He'd cut wood, hauled water, cooked and cleaned, and even on occasion looked after the captain's children. But three months of that was enough, and he was glad when spring came and the arrangement ended. Most of his field work involved escorting emigrant trains and riding through desolate territory so the Saints and potentially hostile Indian tribes would feel the Cavalry's presence.

There was no Sherman family after their father died, or so Ed had thought. Jake was so quiet that he was not much company, and since the family scattered, Ed had felt restless. He and Jake had spent every minute together as boys, but had grown apart as Jake became more introspective and spent more time away from home. Most of the time he was off hunting or scouting or hobnobbing with trappers and Indians. Having a family like that was no good.

Then Captain Byington had taken over command of the fort, and a few months later his daughter arrived to keep him company. Ed had to ride out with a detachment a couple of days later to support settlers in an Indian scare. When he came back a month later, he learned to his surprise that Jake had not only met Laura Byington, but had formed an attachment with her.

Next thing he knew, Jake was married to the captain's daughter. It had stunned him. Laura Byington was revered by every man in the territory, but considered unattainable. Jake had snared her somehow. Or maybe she had caught him, Ed wasn't exactly sure. But shortly after that Ed had asked to continue duty at Fort Bridger, mostly to be near Jake and regain a sense of family.

Laura had encouraged him to visit them often, and he'd found that having a family again was comforting. Jake wasn't as antisocial as he'd once been, and he laughed a lot these days. The little ranch house was warm and cozy again. Laura obviously doted on her husband, without smothering him. And Jake loved it.

Ed wondered if he could ever feel that way about a woman. The frightened girl at Zale's flashed into his mind again. Laura had talked about Iris a lot on the trail today. She hated leaving the girl there, and Ed did, too. She was vulnerable, and she needed someone to stand up for her. His heart went out to her, but could he love someone like that? He pictured a girl with a little more starch to her. Someone like Laura, who rode like a Sioux and dared to back-talk the captain.

Still, he couldn't shake the image of Iris Perkins. He couldn't really tell if she was pretty or not in the dim hen house. Her eyes were large and expressive, but she was so frightened, it was impossible to say what her true personality was like.

He thought about getting up and going out to check the horses. Occasionally he heard a *whack,* and was sure it was Blaze kicking the wall. But if he went out there the dogs would raise a ruckus, and he didn't want to wake Philip. At last he drowsed off.

Chapter 16

The sight of the snug little house Jake's father had built near the Black Fork, with the log barn nestled up to it and the sprawling corrals beyond, was heavenly. Laura's joy and relief bubbled up inside her, and she laughed out loud.

Jake looked over at her from the sorrel stallion's back. "Happy to be home, angel?"

"Ecstatic." She didn't care if Edward saw how much she cared about her new home, or how much she loved her husband. She was in her element now, and the dreary land of Deseret was far behind. She was determined to forget the misery she had seen there.

They had left the Glucks' ranch early, and it took most of the day to travel home, leading the string of mares, her father's new mount, and Shakespeare, but they'd pressed forward eagerly. The sun was dropping behind them when the horses jogged into the door yard.

Laura noticed that Ed and Jake looked around quickly, sizing up the homestead. When they left for a few days, they had no assurance the ranch would not be disturbed while they were gone. She'd heard stories of past raids by Indians, outlaws, and even a marauding grizzly, while Jake was out scouting for the army. But today the little house was peaceful, and everything was in place.

Jake dismounted and pushed the corral gate open, leading the sorrel stallion inside. Laura sat astride Spook outside, just looking at the homey scene. The mountain backdrop was breathtaking at sunset.

Ed turned the horses without saddles loose in the corral, and the two men began unsaddling their mounts.

"Gathering wool, sweetheart?" Jake called.

Laura smiled. "Just storing up memories for later." She swung her leg over the saddle's cantle and hopped down, only a little stiff. She was so used to riding long days now, she wasn't sure what she'd do when Jake settled in for the winter and she was expected to stay at home for weeks on end.

Spook tugged at the reins, pulling her toward the river.

"He's thirsty," Laura said. "I'm going to let him get a drink."

"Best unbridle first."

Jake was particular about the tack, and Laura knew he was right. Leather goods weren't easy to replace. She reached for the buckle on the saddle bag, where she'd stowed Spook's halter that morning. The sound of drumming hoofbeats distracted her.

"Hey! Hal!" Jake grinned as Hal Coleman rode up swiftly from the path to Fort Bridger on his bay mare, Lady.

"Welcome back!"

"Thanks. Tell me what you think." Jake nodded toward the sorrel stallion he'd just set free in the corral, and Hal sat gazing at the horse for several seconds.

Slowly he nodded. "I'd say you've done yourself proud, Jake."

"My assessment as well." Jake reached for a bucket. "What do you think of those mares?"

"Best looking horseflesh I've seen in months." Hal shook his head in wonder. "They been fattening them up in Utah?"

"Apparently so."

"We had to pay for what we got," Ed put in.

"Well, it'll turn out for the best in the long run." Hal nodded with satisfaction as he surveyed the new horses again. "Did the mares come with the sorrel?"

"No," Jake laughed, "but don't tell him that. He's king of the herd already." The stallion pranced about the corral, edging first one mare then another away from the fence.

"He's in top form," Ed said. "Thinks he's got to protect all the mares from us. But he doesn't care much for Spook."

"Oh, they don't get along?" Hal chuckled.

Laura shook her head. "I couldn't ride next to Jake at all today, or Blaze would take a chunk out of Spook's neck."

"The gray gelding's for the captain," Ed said. "Think he'll like him?"

"He looks a little like Spook," Hal said. "Not as tall, but he's sturdy."

"I rode him a little. He's got a really smooth trot." Ed lifted the saddle from Tramp's back. "How's things at Bridger?"

"The usual. You didn't get any remounts for us?"

"They want too much." Ed shrugged.

"Father will understand," Laura said quickly. "I think he expected that, but he wanted Ed to be able to go with us, anyway."

Her father had balked a little when she'd told him Jake wanted to go horse hunting in the Utah territory, and had even blustered a bit when she'd announced that she was going along.

Too dangerous, the captain had said. There was a federal detachment in Utah now, but it was west of Provo, quite a ways from the area Jake intended to scout for breeding stock. But Laura had assured him she was not going to let her husband leave her alone for a week or more while he bartered with the Saints. She was going along, and would help him with the horses that would build their herd and their ranch. That was that.

Once it was established that they were going, Captain Byington had assigned Ed to go along in an official capacity. "A little extra security for you," Andrew Byington had said to his daughter. "And it won't hurt Jake and his brother to have some time together."

She was glad now that Ed had been with them. It would have been hard getting all the horses home without him, especially the fractious stallion.

"Wish you could have come along," she said to Hal. It would have kept his mind off the family he'd left behind in Georgia when he joined the Cavalry, if nothing else.

"Hey, watch it!" Hal said sharply.

She spun toward the corral. The sorrel galloped across the small enclosure toward the five-foot rail fence, as if testing it. He ran toward it, then stopped at the last possible instant, whirling away.

Jake dropped his bucket. "Whoa, you idiot horse!"

"Should have tied him, Jake." Ed's voice was edgy with apprehension. Jake climbed the fence and leaped down inside the corral. The other horses milled around him as the red stallion took another run toward the western end of the corral.

"It's too high," Laura said, but even as the words came from her mouth, Blaze flew over the fence, his hooves a good six inches above the top rail.

Hal threw a quick look at Jake, and without a word turned his mare and tore after the stallion, down the trail that led west, toward Echo Canyon.

"Stupid!"

Laura knew Jake was berating himself. He grabbed his saddle from the fence rail and threw it on Shakespeare's back.

"Take Spook," she yelled. "He's still saddled."

Jake ran toward her. "If I'm not back tonight, just button things up and sit tight."

He was off in a flurry of dust.

"I love you," Laura shouted after him. She climbed the fence. All she could see of Jake was a tuft of dust, far down the trail.

Ed hastily saddled one of the new mares, a red roan she had christened Mabel. "This one's fast, and Tramp's too tired. I'd never catch up."

"It's fine," she agreed. Jake's saddle slid off Shakespeare's back, where he'd left it not fastened, and landed in a heap on the ground, and she jumped down and ran to pick it up. While Ed tightened the cinch on the mare, she pulled Jake's canteen and saddlebag off. "Take these. You may not get back tonight. Jake's tinderbox is in here, and some jerky."

Ed nodded and swung up onto the mare's back. Laura ran to the gate and opened it as he approached.

"If we don't get back, tell your father where we are. I don't know if Hal has leave."

She nodded and waved. Mabel pounded down the trail after Spook and Lady. If any of the horses had a chance of catching Blaze, it was Spook, she told herself.

Suddenly it was very quiet. Laura looked back at the corral. Tramp, Shakespeare, her father's new horse, and the three mares were quieting down, poking around at the meager dead grass. She would have to water them all. She decided to haul the water in buckets, rather than try to maneuver the horses in and out of the gate one at a time. She wished she were chasing after Jake, but then who would take care of the livestock?

Jake had ridden off with her hairbrush. A lot of good that would do him. She swallowed hard. There wasn't much chance they would be back tonight. She had tried so hard to avoid being left here alone.

The sun plunged behind the mountains, and the sky went ruby red in the west for a long moment, then black.

Chapter 17

Ed pushed the mare hard. There was no need to stop and figure out which way the others had gone. The dust from Spook's hooves still floated lazily in the twilight air.

He was torn between keeping on after his brother and heading back. He should report to Captain Byington at the fort, especially if Hal Coleman was going to join Jake on this unexpected pursuit. Ed did not want to go back toward Utah Territory. He'd had enough of it in the last week.

They'd met some nice people. The Glucks were notably hospitable, and there were others who had been fair. But there was always the feeling of distrust and uneasiness.

The girl at Zale's haunted his thoughts.

She'd been frightened. Frightened of being seen with him and Laura. What would the consequences have been, if Isaac Zale had found out Laura had befriended her?

And even before she'd begged them not to tell, she'd been afraid. She hadn't wanted to look at him. He didn't think it was shyness.

Edward wasn't used to being feared. He was fairly quiet, but he was friendly and generally well liked. It bothered him to think a woman would be scared of him. He would never dream of giving her cause for that.

But she'd been on the edge of terror when she'd said, *Do not say that we have spoken, please, Mrs. Sherman.* Yet, she had taken the chance of warning them. She'd known something about the horse.

That he can fly, Ed thought bitterly. They'd been too trusting to figure it out. No doubt Zale had planned on the horse escaping and coming back to him. The thought stoked his ire against Zale.

But the quick anger he felt when he thought about Blaze was nothing compared to the slow, hot wrath that came over him when he remembered Iris's resigned declaration to Laura. *I have no protector now.*

And he had ridden off and left her there.

~~~~~

It was dark, too dark to track. Jake had caught up with Hal within minutes of leaving his ranch. They had entered the area claimed by the Latter Day Saints, and Hal was getting nervous, Jake could see. They passed a burned out house as the last rays of light faded. The bottom half of the chimney stood like a stump, but the upper half had toppled over.

"They burnt that place when they ran from Johnston," Jake noted. "Burned a lot of good crops, too, just to make sure our troops wouldn't get them."

"I know. We had our work cut out for us, building up the fort again."

"It's a lot better now than it was before."

Hal looked over his shoulder. "Gives me the creeps, though, to see an abandoned place like that."

After two hours of backtracking, the long-legged gray horse was still ready to go, although he'd been on the trail all day. Jake thought wryly, *Now, if I could find a stallion with Spook's endurance and personality ...*

"There's a watering place just below here," he called to Hal.

"I recall."

There was no need to keep trying to make out the sorrel's hoof prints. The stallion hadn't been watered before he made his escape, and Jake had already seen that he was making a beeline back down Echo Canyon. He knew Blaze would stop at the stream for a long drink of clear, mountain-cold water.

90

At the place where the trail forded the shallow stream, Jake dismounted and peered long and hard at the tracks. The moon had risen, bright and nearly full. He could see Blaze's prints just fine and read the account easily. The stallion had barreled to the edge of the brook and stood with his front feet in the water long enough for his hind hooves to sink deep in the muddy bank, then splashed across and continued on his way at a more leisurely pace.

"He might join up with a wild band," Hal said doubtfully, looking down at Jake from the saddle.

"No. He knows where he's going." Jake pulled Spook's head up and prepared to mount.

"Maybe we ought to go back, and follow him in the morning."

Jake squinted up at his friend. "You go back. No doubt you're supposed to make a curfew tonight. But it's too far to undo now. I'm going on."

Hal shrugged. "What's the sense, Jake? If he's going back to his former owner, he'll still be there in a couple of days."

"I just don't like it. There's a slim chance I can catch up with him before he's back on his home range. If not, well, I just want to settle this as quickly as possible."

Hal sniffed and looked up at the stars. "Laura's likely worried."

Jake frowned. He hated catching her unaware with a sudden separation, but the whole business felt suspicious. "Zale knew the horse would do this."

"You think so?" Hal seemed mildly surprised.

Jake nodded with conviction. "There was a girl there, at his place, name of Iris. She told Laura to warn me to be careful. We all speculated on what she meant. Now I know."

"You think the old man makes a living selling this horse over and over?"

"Hard to say. I don't suppose he'd do it to his brethren, but he was awfully balky when I asked for a bill of sale. Ed thought he might even accuse me of stealing the horse before we got him out of Utah."

There were faint hoofbeats in the distance, coming from the east.

"There's your brother," Hal said.

"You go back," Jake told him again. "Tell the captain what happened. He didn't pin Ed down on when he was due back. A couple of days, and this will be over. And take that gray we bought from Gluck to him. Maybe that will mollify him until we get back."

Hal hesitated as Ed approached the stream.

"Hey! Jake! That you?"

Jake turned toward the approaching horseman and called lazily, "It's me, all right. That knot-headed stud's tearing for Zale's place, like I figured."

"We going to go on all night? I'm beat." Ed brought Mabel up close to the other horses and dismounted.

"Tell you what," said Hal. "Let's camp here. No sense going on in the pitch dark. Anything could happen. I'll head back first thing in the morning and tell Captain Byington what happened. You two can go on and fetch the horse back."

Jake sighed heavily. He didn't want to wait, but he knew he was too tired to stay alert. If they went on into the inhospitable territory and met with an accident or hostile Indians, or even unfriendly whites, where would that leave Laura? He didn't want to put her through any more harrowing experiences if he could help it.

"Hal's right," Ed said.

"I'll go see Laura before I go to the fort, and get the captain's new horse," Hal promised.

"All right, all right." Jake looked around, evaluating what he could see of the terrain and what he remembered from their passage over the ford early that day. "Let's find a spot to unload and see if we've got anything edible."

Chapter 18

Iris lay in the dark listening for a long time before she carefully sat up and struck a light. She set the candlestick on the floor beside the bed.

Soon she would be leaving the small room she shared with Betsy and Catherine. Isaac and his sons had been working hard to add two rooms to the back of the house, and Eleanor had informed her that after the wedding the newlyweds would share what was now Eleanor's bedchamber. The new rooms would become Eleanor's new sitting room and bedchamber.

Iris wondered how that had come about. Delia was fuming. She snapped at Iris and the girls for any reason or no reason, and she was sharp tongued to everyone in the family except her husband. Eleanor went about her housework quietly, but with a satisfied expression. She had an inner strength that Iris hadn't suspected. No, things were not going Delia's way.

As the wedding day approached, a cloud of gloom settled over Iris. She was glad Rufus was so busy with the building and farm work. Once again tonight she had avoided the hated parlor sitting. The men were pushing themselves to get the new addition finished, and they went back at it after supper. Iris made her exit from the kitchen as soon as the dishes were washed. She had heard Isaac and his sons come in an hour later, but the girls were already getting ready for bed, and no one came to tell her she had to go downstairs, so she went to bed, too, with a sense of reprieve.

But the wedding was coming. She was sure Isaac would not allow another postponement. She felt desperately that there was something she must do, something she must learn, before that day came. But no one in the Zale family seemed able or willing to tell her what that was. And so she turned to the little leather-covered book Laura Sherman had given her.

Iris didn't dare read the New Testament often, for fear she would be discovered. She had decided that it was safest to read it in the bedroom, where Zale and his sons never intruded, but late at night, when the girls were asleep.

She sat still for several seconds, watching the girls. Even in repose, Catherine looked fretful. Betsy worried her more, however. She'd come weeping to Iris the day before with a tale of teasing by her brothers. Luke had taunted her to tears, calling her skinny and homely, and then Elmer had said, *Don't bother with her, Luke. Pa will give her to an elder soon, and we won't have to look at her any longer.*

The shocking words had stunned Iris, and she had no comfort for the terrified girl.

Now she stealthily removed the little book from the pocket of her housedress. In Ephesians, Chapter 5, she had found another passage Laura had marked, concerning marriage, and she wanted to read it again. When she tried to fit the words with what she saw among the Latter Day Saints, some of it held up—wives in submission, husbands as head of the house—but there were other parts that just didn't seem to ring true to what she saw.

Husbands, love your wives, even as Christ also loved the church, and gave himself for it...So ought men to love their wives as their own bodies.

Oh, Brother Zale loved his body, all right. He made sure it was fed and clothed and sheltered. But did he show that same love to Delia and Eleanor?

Iris pondered that and decided he did provide for his wives and children. It was a hard life out here, and Zale was diligent in building up his ranch. They were never hungry. But love? Was that all love was, providing the necessities? She didn't think so. *As Christ also loved the church.* Christ had done much more than put wood in the stove and beef on the table.

"What are you reading?"

94

Iris jumped and instinctively tried to hide the book below the edge of the bed. Betsy sat up, blinking at her.

"What is it?"

Iris drew a deep breath. "It's—it's Scripture."

Betsy's eyes flew open. "Not Pa's book."

"No."

"Where did you get it?"

"A friend gave it to me."

Betsy eyed her dubiously, and Iris knew the girl would have known of the book's existence if she'd had it the full month they'd lived together.

"You won't—" Iris stopped. She hated to ask Betsy not to tell, as it was tantamount to advising her to disobey her parents.

"What does it say?" Betsy drew her knees up and folded her arms around them, leaning eagerly toward Iris.

"Lots of things."

"Like what?"

"Oh, well, like … *Children obey your parents.*"

Betsy's eyes turned upward in exasperation. "Everyone knows that. What else?"

"It—it tells about Jesus. And, well, *lots* of things."

"You said that."

Iris sighed.

Betsy asked tentatively, "Does it say anything about what to do when you're in trouble, or bad things are happening to you?"

"I haven't had time to read it all." Iris watched her face, trying to decide whether Betsy would betray her.

"Read some to me." The younger girl's face was so wistful, that Iris couldn't refuse.

"All right, but come closer. We have to be really quiet." It was very cold in the bedroom, and Iris put the candle back up on the bedside table and huddled under the quilts again, close to Betsy. She wasn't sure she wanted to read the part about husbands and wives to Betsy, so she flipped back a few pages, scanning quickly.

95

"Here's something my friend marked. *Therefore, seeing we have this ministry, as we have received mercy, we faint not, but have renounced the hidden things of dishonesty, not walking in craftiness, nor—*"

"Pa thinks it's good to be crafty," Betsy interrupted.

Iris eyed her cautiously. It would not do to speak ill of the girl's father and her future father-in-law. At last she said quietly, "Well, he's a clever man, that's for sure."

"Is it dishonest to sell a man a ewe that you know is barren?"

Iris shifted uneasily. Two weeks earlier, Isaac had boasted at the dinner table over the way he had unloaded three barren ewes in a flock of twenty he sold for breeding stock. "I—" She stopped short, having no answer.

Betsy shrugged. "Read some more."

"*Nor handling the word of God deceitfully, but by manifestation of the truth, commending ourselves to every man's conscience in the sight of God.*" Betsy settled back on the pillow, her eyes focusing on the board ceiling above, her brows drawn together in a frown.

"What does that mean?"

"I'm not sure. That we should always be honest with every man, I guess."

"But we're not."

Iris stared at her. "What do you mean?" she whispered, not sure she wanted an answer.

"Pa takes advantage of anyone he can, and Ma doesn't tell him half the stuff the boys do when he's gone. Elmer lies all the time, and Rufus is the worst. You know when he was gone all one night, and he told Pa his horse took lame and he stayed with those folks near Castle Rock?"

Iris nodded.

"He didn't really. I heard him telling Luke later, and Luke promised not to tell Pa."

Iris blinked. "So, where was he? Nay, don't tell me." She sighed and lay back on her pillow.

"Aren't you going to read anymore?"

"You want me to?"

"Yes."

Iris raised the book again so she could see the words in the candlelight. *"But if our gospel be hidden, it is hidden to them that are lost, in whom the god of this world hath blinded the minds of them who believe not, lest the light of the glorious gospel of Christ, who is the image of God, should shine on them. For we preach not ourselves, but Christ Jesus the Lord, and ourselves your servants for Jesus' sake. For God, who commanded the light to shine out of darkness, hath shined in our hearts, to give the light of the knowledge of the glory of God in the face of Jesus Christ. But we have this treasure in earthen vessels, that the excellency of the power may be of God, and not of us."*

Iris stopped reading. "It's too hard to understand," she sighed. "All of this about Jesus Christ ... I don't know what it means. It says God's light shines in our hearts, but I don't have any light or knowledge."

"Maybe you need to study more," Betsy said, her eyes wide in innocence.

Iris smiled. "Maybe so. I think that's enough for tonight."

"Just a little more," Betsy begged.

"All right."

"I wish you were my sister," Betsy whispered, pulling the quilt up close around her chin.

"Do you?" Iris considered that, wondering if it would be less horrible to be Isaac Zale's daughter than to be Rufus's wife.

"If you were my sister, you could stay here with Catherine and me. But if you marry Rufus, you have to go live downstairs."

Iris swallowed hard. "Let's read." She blinked back the tears that were forming in her eyes and found her place. *"We are troubled on every side, yet not distressed; we are perplexed, but not in despair; persecuted, but not forsaken; cast down, but not destroyed."*

"That's us!" Betsy cried, sitting bolt upright.

"Sh!" Iris looked over at Catherine, but she slept on peacefully. Straining to hear any sounds of movement in the house, she tried to quiet her pounding heart.

"Sorry." Betsy's shoulders drooped.

"It's all right, but I think we'd better blow out the candle. If your Pa sees a light or hears us—"

"We'll be in trouble." Betsy snuggled down under the covers while Iris tucked the book under her pillow and snuffed the candle. "But it *is* us," she whispered when Iris lay beside her. "We're troubled and perplexed. And the saints are persecuted wherever they go. Even here, they sent the Army after us."

"Perplexed, but not in despair ... cast down, but not destroyed." Iris closed her eyes tight.

"I'm perplexed," said Betsy.

Iris almost laughed. "What about, honey?"

Betsy's head nestled against her shoulder. "About what Elmer said. Would Pa really give me in marriage, do you think?"

"I hope not. Not yet. And when he does, I hope it's to a nice young man who will love you and take care of you."

"I don't get to meet many nice young men." It was a simple statement of fact, but its pathos pulled at Iris's heart.

"I know."

"You don't, either. You only get to meet the people the elders say you can, and then they give you to a boy you don't even know."

Iris had no answer.

"Why do some men in Zion have lots of wives, and some don't have any?" Betsy asked.

"I don't know." Iris wished she would stop talking. What would Betsy say if she told her, *I met a nice young man yesterday. His name is Edward Sherman, and he was concerned about me.* No, she must never tell anyone, never speak his name aloud.

"Remember," Betsy said, "whatever happens, we're troubled, but we're not—not—what came next?"

"Distressed."

"That's right," Betsy said brightly. "We're not distressed." After a moment, she added uncertainly, "Are we?"

98

Iris reached over and caught the girl's hand and squeezed it. "We're not distressed," she repeated. "We're cast down, but not destroyed."

"Yes," Betsy breathed. "That's us. Not destroyed. But, Iris?"

"What?"

Betsy yawned. "What does it mean, not forsaken?"

"We're not alone, I guess."

Betsy was quiet, and Iris thought she had drifted off to sleep, but suddenly she whispered, "I suppose that could mean there are lots of women like us. We're not alone."

"No!" That interpretation was too bleak for Iris to accept. Her pulse began to race as she mentally fought the idea.

"What does it mean, then?"

"I think ... well, I'm not certain, but remember before that, how it talked about God's light shining in our hearts?"

"No," Betsy admitted.

"Well, I think it means God hasn't forsaken us."

"Oh."

They lay still, and soon Betsy's even breathing told Iris that the girl slept at last. She lay awake for a long time, staring into the blackness, toward the one crack of gray that told her where the edge of the shuttered window was. The tears came freely now, cooling as they ran down her cheeks in the chilly air, but she did not wipe them away. She wished desperately that Laura Sherman were here and could explain the mysterious verses she had underlined in the book.

She would have to find the spot when it was daylight and read it again. If only she could have hope that, no matter what happened to her, she would not be forsaken or destroyed.

Chapter 19

Iris awoke suddenly, her heart pounding. As she grabbed a breath, she realized that there was more pounding outside. A horse was galloping into the barnyard at full tilt. Even as she grasped the fact, she heard footsteps in the house below her, and in the room next door the three boys hit the floor.

With shaking hands, she reached for the candlestick, but realized she couldn't make a light. Whoever was outside would see the glow from her window, even behind the curtains. Flinging back the quilts, she dashed to the wall. She fumbled to lower the shutter panel that covered the whole open hole that was their window, praying the hinge at the bottom wouldn't creak.

In the full moonlight, she saw the sorrel stallion standing before the barn door, his head down and his sides heaving. The dogs were barking, and the horses in the pasture were galloping in circles, neighing and kicking up their heels. Isaac Zale ran out the kitchen doorway, a rifle in his hand, and his sons pelted after him. Isaac was wearing his boots and trousers, but the boys wore only their union suits.

Isaac stopped short when he spotted the horse. His hearty laugh rang out in the frosty night. "Well, well, look who's come home."

Rufus ran gingerly across the yard in his bare feet and grasped the horse's halter. "What are we gonna do with him, Pa?"

"Do?" Isaac roared. "Tie him up in the barn, of course." He laughed again, and Iris shivered. Silently she raised the shutter and turned the wooden blocks that held it in place, then felt her way back to the bed.

"What is it?" Betsy whispered.

"The stallion is back."

"Red?"

"Yes."

Betsy took a deep, shaky breath. "I hope the man who bought him is all right."

"Me, too." A sudden, sickening thought struck her. "Is that horse trained to come back?"

"I don't know if he's exactly trained," Betsy said, "but he always does."

"Your father will have to give Mr. Sherman his money back."

"Oh, he never does that."

A cold chill ran through Iris, and she pulled the quilt up under her chin. She didn't want to know how Brother Zale managed that.

Betsy seemed inclined to tell her, anyway. "The last time, the widow came with her father."

"Widow?" Iris squeaked.

"Red kicked her husband in the head. Pa told her the horse must have gone crazy, and was too dangerous for her to handle, but he'd give her a nice, quiet mare instead. Her pa didn't like it, but my pa wouldn't give over any money or take any blame."

"So they took the mare?"

"Yes. I think they were scared not to."

"No doubt."

"And it was the sorriest plug you ever saw. But they seemed glad to leave by that time."

Iris heard the boys climbing the stairs, and Betsy leaped out of bed. She flung the door open just as Luke and Elmer reached the landing.

"What did Pa do with Red?" she demanded.

"Put him in the barn, Miss Nosy," Elmer replied.

"Are we keeping him?"

The boys looked at each other in the light of Elmer's candle, and Luke laughed. "Rufus is taking him to the east meadow at first light."

"But you didn't hear that," Elmer whispered with a threat in his voice.

"You didn't hear anything," Luke added. "You slept peacefully all night and didn't hear any horses running around at midnight."

Betsy closed the door silently and walked stiffly back to the bed. She plopped down on her side, saying nothing. Iris wanted to speak to her, to give comfort and an explanation that would show how nothing was wrong, but she couldn't.

Catherine wriggled on her little cot. "Betsy?" she said sleepily. "What's going on?"

"Nothing," said Betsy.

"Is it time to get up?"

"No. Go back to sleep."

Betsy slid beneath the covers, and Iris reached out to her, pulling her over next to her.

"We are troubled on every side, yet not distressed," she whispered.

"We are perplexed, but not in despair," Betsy's response came immediately.

"We can pray about this," Iris said. She felt suddenly timid.

"Yes," Betsy agreed. "There's nothing else we can do, is there?"

"I suppose not." Long before her silent, anguished prayer was finished, Iris knew Betsy was once more asleep. *Dear God, help me! How can I live like this? How can I promise to be a faithful wife to this man? I would rather die than marry Rufus Zale.* She sobbed silently into her pillow.

In her reading of the book of Titus at Laura's suggestion, she had found the words, *Ordain elders in every city ... if any be blameless, the husband of one wife, having faithful children not accused of riot, or unruly.* She couldn't see that Brother Zale could meet any of those qualifications. And yet, she was expected to revere him and marry his son.

"I can't," she whispered in anguish. "Dear God, I can't. Please don't forsake me now. The Bible says I can be perplexed, but not in despair. Lord, I *am* in despair! Is it because I don't have your light shining in my heart?"

She lay still for a long, long time, hearing the boys' bunks creak as they rolled over, and the restless stomping of the stallion in the barn. Rufus came up the stairs and went into the boys' room, and she could hear Luke and Elmer peppering him with questions. Cold as it was, Iris crept out of bed and pressed her ear to the wall.

Chapter 20

Laura woke before dawn. She threw back the covers and left the comfortless bed. Hugging herself and rubbing her arms for warmth, she ran to the kitchen and looked out at the silent yard. The horses were moving about in the corral. Their breath sent up little clouds of vapor when they snorted.

She built up the fire in the stove and wondered if the men were sleeping on the frozen ground. For an hour she kept busy, feeding and watering the horses, making coffee and biscuits, and starting a stew that could simmer on the back of the stove until Jake came home.

She sat down at the kitchen table with a biscuit, a cup of coffee, and the Sherman family Bible, the one Jake's parents had brought from Massachusetts. She and Jake had made a habit of reading from it at breakfast. She turned to the Psalms.

Slowly her agitation eased as she read. *For thou wilt light my candle; the Lord, my God, will lighten my darkness. For by thee I have run through a troop; and by my God have I leaped over a wall.* She smiled involuntarily at the image of the fiery red horse flying over the fence. All right, Blaze, she thought, You're not the only one who can leap walls. *As for God, his way is perfect; the word of the Lord is tried; he is a buckler to all those who trust in him.*

"Lord, I trust you," she prayed. "Guide me now, in your wisdom."

She sat quietly for a few moments, calming herself, ready to wait or to act. Then she rose with another swift prayer. In the bedroom, she put on her warmest woolen stockings, her riding skirt, a fresh shirtwaist, a sweater, and her warm coat.

"Come on, Shakespeare, get over here," she called as she carried Jake's saddle to the corral. Shakespeare eyed her balefully and snorted, his breath escaping his nostrils in white plumes.

Laura sighed and climbed the fence. Shakespeare was docile enough and let her catch him, even though he wouldn't make it easy for her by coming to her call. She saddled him quickly and removed his halter, drawing the bridle up over his long face.

~~~~~

Jake dumped the dregs from the single tin coffee cup he had shared with Ed and Hal for their early breakfast and pulled on his leather gloves. The three were huddled over a small campfire, absorbing its meager warmth. "Let's get this over with."

Ed nodded and kicked the embers of the fire apart, then emptied the coffee pot on them.

With cold, stiff fingers, they quickly packed up their few implements and readied the horses. Clouds had rolled in after midnight, and no stars were showing in the predawn sky.

"Take care, Jake," Hal said as he swung onto Lady's back.

Jake frowned. "You tell the captain the story. If I'm not back by tomorrow sundown, maybe he'd consider sending a few men out to Echo Canyon the next morning."

Hal nodded soberly. "You wouldn't go alone, just the two of you, if you expected real trouble, would you, Jake?"

Jake grimaced. "Truthfully, I don't know what to expect. Right now, I'm just assuming I bought a horse that's part fox and part falcon."

Hal nodded and looked at Ed. "God speed."

Ed nodded.

Jake turned Spook westward and didn't look back.

~~~~~

They rode silently for an hour in the frigid morning, loping whenever the terrain allowed.

"Feels like snow," Ed said at last.

His brother didn't turn in the saddle, but rode on with his back straight. Ed decided he hadn't heard. They approached the opening of the canyon, and the hoofbeats echoed eerily, like the pounding of carpenters banging away on boards.

When the trail widened out, Ed urged Mabel up beside Spook. The first crisp flakes were drifting down.

"We don't want to get snowed in this side of the pass," Ed said.

Jake's face was like granite. "We'll get back."

"What if we don't?"

Jake looked at him, and Ed could see he was holding back anger and frustration.

"Breathe, Jake."

Jake exhaled with what might have been a chuckle. "Yes, mother."

They both laughed. It was their sister, Vivian, who had held her breath when she got angry as a child, and their mother would dispassionately say, "Breathe, Vivian Isabel," and then walk away.

"You caught me," Jake admitted. "I've been trying not to argue with the Lord about this, but I can't understand it. Why would He let this crazy thing happen?"

Ed shook his head. "I don't know, but He has."

Jake sighed. "Must be trying to teach me patience or something. The last place I want to be today is Zale's ranch."

"Me, too," Ed said, but even as he said it, an idea whispered into his mind. "Of course, there might be something good come of it."

"Like what?"

"Well ... there's that girl. Iris Perkins."

Jake looked hard at him. "You mean the only reason you tagged along is because you might get another peek at that girl?"

"No! I'd help you, no matter what, but ... Jake, she's in an awful fix."

"Can't help it."

Ed struggled for a moment, thought better of what he wanted to say, then said it anyway. "Jake, if there's any way we can help her—"

"No. N-O." Jake's evident annoyance made Ed feel much younger than his brother. He was four years Jake's junior, and all his life he'd tried to catch up.

"Look, don't you think it's possible God wants us to go back there for a reason?"

Jake shook his head. "If we say anything about the girl, it will just make Zale mad. He'll run us off, then take it out on her."

Ed winced. "Well, he's going to be mad, anyway. Just seeing us ride in will likely make him mad. And if the stallion is there and he doesn't want us to take it, he'll be furious."

Jake threw him a dark look. "At least you've got your rifle. I came off without mine."

"You really think we'll need to defend ourselves?"

"I don't know."

"Well, we've got our revolvers."

Jake grunted. "We're going to do everything possible to make this a peaceful visit. And that doesn't include offering to take that girl off Zale's hands."

"But, Jake, they're making her marry a man against her will. That's illegal."

Jake nodded. "So's polygamy. So's fraud. So's a lot of things. You think that's going to stop him?"

Ed rode on in silence, but his troubled thoughts were churning. He didn't know as he could ride up out of Echo Canyon a second time knowing Iris Perkins was still at Zale's. She'd looked so defenseless. So earnest, so resolute. Like a martyr.

"I can't leave her there, Jake."

Jake's head snapped around, and his jaw dropped. He pulled Spook to a halt and sat staring at him.

Ed licked his wind-chapped lips and wished he hadn't. "I'm sorry, I just can't. It's not right."

Jake took a deep breath. "Look, Edward, it's going to be hard enough getting the horse back. You can't just carry off a man's betrothed."

"Betrothed! That is a joke, and you know it. It's a crime, brother, and that girl is the victim. If he were beating her, would you take your precious horse and ride away, telling me, *It's none of our business? Would you?*"

Jake ran a hand over his stubbly chin. "I knew I should have sent you back with Hal. I just had a feeling."

Ed raised his chin. "Quit it. I'm not six years old. I'll stand by you in this. You can't go alone, and you know it. You can't trust that old geezer. You need me, Jake."

Jake leaned forward, crossing his hands on the saddle horn, and sighed. "Sure wish I'd stopped long enough to change the saddles."

Edward laughed.

"All right." Jake's brown eyes, normally placid, were fierce now. "I know how I'd feel if Laura was in a bad spot. I guess you can't help it. What do you suggest we do?"

Ed smiled. His brother did understand, after all. "We ride in calm and quiet, and we ask him about the horse. If things go well, we mention that your wife asked us to invite Miss Perkins to come for a visit."

Jake shook his head vigorously. "Never work. They're getting married next week, idiot. You think they'll let her leave the territory to visit a gentile woman the week before the wedding? You're nuts."

Ed knew he was right. He moved Mabel into a trot, and they rode on in silence, along Needle Creek past a ridge of high, jagged rocks, and then the approach to Cache Cave. He'd explored it last fall with the other men in a patrol detachment.

"There'll be a stagecoach line through here soon," he said.

Jake scowled. "They'll have to do a sight of work on this so-called road."

"Well, the word at the fort is, they're building the line from Salt Lake to San Francisco this year. It won't be long before they bring it on through." The idea of being able to ride in a stagecoach clear across the continent excited Ed. The land was being civilized, like it or not.

Jake just grunted, and Ed knew he didn't welcome the thought of more and more people going through the Green River Valley. After several minutes of silence, Jake said, "Zale might tell us the horse never showed up there. Then what do we do?"

Ed exploded in pent-up exasperation. "Oh, the horse, the horse! All you care about is the horse!"

Jake's hurt showed in his mournful expression. "That's why we're here in the first place, remember?"

"Yes, but we may not get the horse back. Have you considered that?"

"Yes. If Zale lies about it, we won't be able to disprove what he says. And if that stallion truly didn't go back to him, there's not much we can do about it. The ground's frozen hard now. We're not likely to find any more tracks."

"Iris said he sets a lot of store by that horse."

"Meaning?"

"Who knows. But maybe, just maybe, he likes the horse more than he likes Iris. Is that possible?"

Jake shook his head. "Not the same thing at all, little brother."

"What if we offer to make him a trade?"

"Are you insane?" Spook flinched at Jake's shout, and he patted the horse's flank. "Sorry, fella." He shook his head and eyed Ed in disbelief. "A man does not trade his daughter-in-law for a horse, even his favorite horse."

"She's not his daughter-in-law." Ed was startled at the grimness of his own voice.

Jake cocked his head to one side. "As good as."

"Whoa!" Ed reached out and grasped Spook's reins just below the bit and pulled both horses to a stop.

"What now?" Jake was bristling with irritation.

"Don't say things like that, all right? She is not married to young Zale yet. I've been praying, and I know Laura has too, for the last two days, that God will somehow stop that wedding. Well, maybe we're the answer to those prayers."

110

Jake took two deep breaths. "Let go of the reins, Ed."
Slowly, Ed unclenched his fist and released Spook.

"All right." Jake sat still for a moment. "Look, we need to get there fast, so let's not argue. This snow looks like it means business, and you know Brother Zale won't want to put us up tonight. Just pray while we're getting there, understand? If the Lord gives us an opening—if we see her, or if the old man isn't around, say—maybe we can speak up and ask her straight out if she wants to leave."

"I know she wants to leave." Ed knew at that instant that if Iris did not leave with them, he would never rest easy again.

Suddenly Jake's head jerked up, and he pulled Spook in short. Ed halted his horse and turned his face to the west, listening. The hammering of hoofbeats was faint, then echoed loud above them, off the high canyon walls.

Chapter 21

Laura tied Shakespeare to the hitching post in front of her father's office and strode quickly inside. Corporal Markheim jumped to his feet, and her father looked up from writing at his desk.

"The party has returned safely, I take it?" Andrew Byington asked.

"Well, yes and no." Laura put her arms around him and kissed his cheek. "Has Private Coleman come back yet?"

"Coleman? I didn't know he was gone."

"He came to the house last evening, just as we returned home. Father, the stallion Jake bought got loose, and he and Ed and Hal Coleman went after him."

The captain sat down again, frowning. "They're out chasing a stallion?"

"Yes, but he's not a wild stallion. Jake bought him from a rancher beyond Echo Canyon. He's beautiful and strong, and his conformation is perfect."

Captain Byington nodded. "But he ran off."

"Yes!" Laura pounded her father's desk in exasperation. "He took the corral fence. You've seen Jake's fence. It's sturdy and high. I wouldn't believe it if I hadn't been there to see it."

"Sounds like a good steeplechase horse."

"Oh, Father, Jake looked so amazed and so sick when that horse made his break. Private Coleman was mounted, and he went after the stallion immediately, and Jake and Ed followed him. I hardly slept last night, I was so worried."

"Sit down, Laura Margaret. Worrying won't help things, child."

"I know. I sorted that out with God this morning, and I decided to come tell you and see if Private Coleman came back last night. Jake thought he might."

Andrew Byington leaned forward and called to the corporal, "Markheim, go see if Private Coleman is in the fort."

"Yes, sir." Markheim went out, and Laura pulled a chair close to her father's desk.

"He's just the horse Jake wanted, as far as looks go, but he's fretful. Wanted to run all the way. Jake had to work hard to keep him in line. And we hadn't been home ten minutes when he escaped."

"Did they head up into the mountains?"

"No, back toward Utah territory." Laura sighed and rested her chin on her hand, leaning on the corner of the desk. "We have reason to think he's headed back to his home ranch."

"How's that?"

"A girl who was staying with the family warned Ed and me that Jake should be careful. We didn't know what she meant, but ... Jake's got the idea that horse is a trickster."

"I see."

She sighed. "Jake paid a lot of money for him. At least he insisted on a bill of sale. But he left in such a hurry, he didn't take it with him, and I'm afraid that might cause some trouble." She reached into her pocket and drew out a folded half sheet of paper. "Will you keep it for me? Put it in your safe?"

"Of course." Byington took it and laid it on top of the desk. "We'll see if we can sort things out. Could you lead a detachment to that ranch if necessary?"

"Easy as pie."

"All right. Let's see if there's any word yet."

The captain rose and went to the door of his cramped headquarters. The chill wind blew in when he opened it, and Laura drew her wool coat closer.

"Markheim!" her father shouted. Laura caught the faint reply.

"He's just riding in, sir."

114

"Well, take his horse and send him in here." The captain sounded a bit gruff, and Laura hoped she hadn't let Hal in for some discipline. Once again her impetuosity seemed to have made a bad situation worse. If she'd stayed home this morning, her father wouldn't have known Hal was out all night.

A moment later Coleman was saluting just inside the doorway, breathing hard. Fresh snowflakes on his hat and shoulders melted away in seconds.

"At ease, Coleman. What happened last night? Is my son-in-law all right?"

"Yes, sir. At least he was at first light. I left him and Ed at the Swift Branch, where we camped last night. The horse was definitely headed that way. Jake figures he bolted for home, and he's going back to Zale's to see if the horse has turned up there." He glanced apologetically at Laura. "I stopped by your place, but I guess you'd already left to come here. Hope you don't mind, I brought the captain's new mount along."

"What's this?" Andrew Byington asked.

"Ed bought a nice gelding for you, Father," Laura said. "I'm sorry I forgot to tell you. I was too distracted by this other business." She turned to Hal. "Thanks for bringing him over. I wasn't sure I could handle an extra horse by myself."

Byington stood looking hard at Hal for a moment. "I suppose you had leave last night."

"Yes, sir. But I should have come back before midnight, sir." Hal stared straight ahead.

"Father, please don't hold it against Private Coleman. If you'd been there and the only one at the ready, you'd have given chase, too."

The captain raised his hand slightly, and Laura took that to mean she should be silent. She clamped her lips tight together.

"I have a message for you, sir." Hal said.

"Speak."

"Jake asked, if he's not back by sundown tomorrow, could you possibly send a few men out? He's not looking for trouble, sir, but he's thinking he might find it anyway. He's also thinking you'll excuse his brother for a couple more days to help him out."

Byington turned his back to Coleman, studying the large territorial map on the wall behind his desk. Laura sat still, trying not to fidget. When her father was her father, he was approachable and even jolly or tender at times. But when he was the captain, he could be quite stern. She saw his head turn slightly, and she knew he was tracing the route from the Sherman ranch to Echo Canyon.

After a few moments, he turned around. "Did Private Sherman find any horses for our remuda?"

"No, sir. He said the prices were too high. Jake bought four good-looking brood mares, but his brother didn't find anything within the Army's budget." Hal reached inside his uniform jacket and drew out a leather pouch. "Private Sherman gave me this and asked me to return it to you."

Laura knew the pouch held the money her father had entrusted to Ed for the horse buying expedition. The captain took it from Hal's hand.

"All right, Coleman, go get cleaned up and see if you've missed any duties."

Byington sat down when the trooper had left. The lines at the corners of his eyes deepened as he frowned.

Laura pushed back her chair and stood. "I'd better go home, in case they come back today."

"No, give me a minute." Her father's tone was gentle now. "I'm sorry this happened, but it's apt to turn out all right. Don't tie yourself up in knots."

"I'll try not to, Daddy."

He smiled up at her, and she knew she sounded once more like his little girl, afraid of the dark, but trying to keep a stiff upper lip. This time the captain couldn't come into her room and shine his lantern under the bed to prove there were no bears hiding there.

"Let's pray about this together."

Laura sat down again and placed her hand in his. "Thank you, Daddy."

Chapter 22

"Someone's coming," Jake whispered.

Ed sat immobile. "One horse?"

"Hard to tell with all the echoing."

They waited uneasily, and when Ed saw Jake draw his revolver, he pulled his rifle from the scabbard. The snowflakes swirled about them. He was just going to suggest they take cover when Jake hissed, "There!"

Rounding a bend in the trail came a single horse. He was jogging steadily, and his hoofbeats reverberated with a loud clanging as he came closer.

"I'll eat my hat if that's not Blaze," Jake muttered. "Think it's a trick?"

Ed squinted and focused on the rider. It couldn't be. But that was definitely a woman's bonnet.

"It's Iris." He was certain even as he said it. Bundled up in layers of bulky clothing, she was unrecognizable, but something in his heart told him it was her.

Jake sat rigid, waiting, watching the interloper intently.

As Blaze approached them, Spook let out a challenging whinny, and Ed saw the girl look ahead and spot them. She stopped the stallion and sat still for a moment, then lifted one hand in a timid wave.

Ed put the rifle away and urged Mabel down the trail. Jake could follow or not, as he pleased.

Only her eyes showed between the brim of her green wool bonnet and the gray muffler she had wound about her neck and lower face. It was the first time Ed had seen them in daylight, and he caught his breath involuntarily. They were deep brown eyes, with a definite violet cast.

"Iris," he said, still staring at her eyes. No wonder her mother had named her that.

"Mr. Sherman. I thought I might meet you and save you some trouble."

"Much obliged."

"He came home at midnight. I thought perhaps I could get him back to you without ..." She looked nervously over her shoulder.

Jake rode up beside Ed and looked the horse and the girl over. "I really appreciate this, Miss Perkins. I hope you haven't had any trouble because of us."

"Not yet, anyway."

"I take it Brother Zale doesn't know you're doing this." Jake's voice was kind, almost as gentle as the tone he kept for Laura, and Ed had a flicker of hope that his brother was now in full sympathy with Iris, and they would indeed be able to help her.

She pulled the muffler down to her chin. "No, he certainly doesn't. That is, he may have figured it out by now, but I waited until the house was quiet again, then slipped out. No one followed me to the barn. I was afraid the dogs would start barking, but I guess they're used to me now. I led Red out the back way, through the sheep pen, and walked him in the grass until we were well away from the house."

Jake nodded. "The saddle—"

"I regret having to take that, and the bridle, too, but I'm not much of a rider, Mr. Sherman. I knew Red was spunky, and I didn't think I could handle him without. If he'd been well rested, I'm sure I couldn't have stayed on him."

"I'll see that the gear is returned, or send Brother Zale enough to pay for them," Jake said. "I sincerely hope you're not blamed for this, Miss Perkins."

She drew a shaky breath. "I considered my options, sir, and this seemed the best way. If you had come to the house—" She looked quickly at Ed, then back to Jake. "Brother Zale had a plan, and I knew you'd come out the worse."

"What sort of plan?" Jake asked.

She was quiet for a moment. Her bright eyes belied the calmness in her voice. "His oldest son was to take the horse to a hiding place at dawn. I believe he would simply have denied that Red came back and sent you off on a wild goose chase. But I also heard the boys talking, and they had plans to distract you and try to lay hands on your bill of sale, so that you couldn't prove you'd ever paid for the horse."

Ed stared at her. "Surely the whole family wouldn't lie about something like that."

Her long, dark lashes fluttered against her pale cheek. "I cannot say for certain, sir, but that was my impression."

Ed wondered if she had witnessed other incidents of dishonesty in the Zale household. How much had this girl borne in enforced silence during her time with the family?

"They'll miss you first thing," Jake said, and Ed felt his brother was weighing Iris's chances of going unpunished.

"I left a note for Betsy. She's the oldest girl, and we shared a bed. I left it where she would find it. I didn't say I was taking the horse, but at least they'll know I left of my own will. I simply said I couldn't enter into marriage without knowing my father's wishes. If they brand me a thief—well, so be it. I know the horse is yours."

"I owe you a large favor, Miss Perkins."

"Well, that's good, Mr. Sherman, because I'm in need of a favor today."

"Name it," Ed said quickly, smiling down into the lovely, wide violet eyes.

Jake said more cautiously, "If there's anything we can help you with, Miss Perkins ..."

"I do hope you can! There are two things, actually, and I need them badly."

"We'll escort you home, if that's what you want."

Ed stared at Jake but said nothing, realizing he had worded his proposition so that Iris would tell them what her true wishes were.

"It's not what I want. That's not my home." Iris's gaze went back to Ed, and she hesitated. "I was hoping Mrs. Sherman would be with you, and I could ride back to Fort Bridger with you."

The brothers locked eyes for an instant.

"You're welcome to ride with us," Ed offered. "If we hurry, we might just make it back to Bridger by tonight."

Jake studied the sky apprehensively. "This snow will slow us down. We might get caught on the trail overnight, ma'am. I'd hate to put you in an awkward position."

"We could go to the Glucks'," Ed suggested. "It's not far now."

Jake shook his head. "I'd rather not bring them into this. There could be bad feelings over the horse, and even more if Miss Perkins goes with us."

Ed nodded. It would be best all around to get over the line into Wyoming, he was sure.

Jake eyed Iris critically. "Are you certain about this?"

"I am."

"Then I suggest we swap horses right now. I grabbed my wife's horse because he still had his saddle on."

Recognition broke over Iris's face. "That's right. You rode a bay horse."

Jake nodded. "Only trouble is, it's her saddle. I've been pretty uncomfortable. This fella's fast, but he's well mannered. He'll give you an easy ride."

"I'll trust your judgment, Mr. Sherman." She dismounted, and Ed jumped down to hold the stallion while Jake boosted her onto Spook's back and adjusted the stirrups for her. The red stallion pulled at the reins, trying to get within biting range of Spook's flank, and Ed pulled him away a few paces.

"It's a beautiful saddle." Iris's gloved hand stroked the tooled reddish leather of the pommel.

"It was a gift from her father," Jake said as he ran the right stirrup as high as it would go.

"He must love her very much."

"That he does."

"He gave her this, too." Iris reached inside her voluminous cloak and pulled out a tiny leather-bound book.

"Laura's New Testament." Jake raised his eyebrows.

"She gave it to me the other day. She insisted I take it and read it. But that's my second favor, Mr. Sherman. There are things in here that I don't understand." She looked down at him earnestly from the saddle. "I need someone to tell me what it means to have the light of God shining in your heart. Your wife underlined those words, so I figure she understands it."

Ed's heart leaped at her words, and he felt a lump forming in his throat.

Jake grasped the toe of Iris's shoe and eased her foot into the stirrup. "Laura and I will be happy to discuss anything in that book with you, ma'am, but right now I think we'd best make tracks."

"I expect you're right." She held the New Testament out to him.

"You keep that," Jake said. "If you want to, you can return it to Laura yourself, but I think she'll want you to have it."

Ed's admiration for his brother shot up several notches. Jake turned toward him, and Ed handed him the stallion's reins.

"He's not as jumpy as he was yesterday."

"Good," Jake grunted. "I'm kind of glad to see him worn down a bit, if the truth be told. Riding Spook spoils you for any other horse."

Ed mounted and said under his breath, "We'll be leaving an easy trail to read in this snow."

Jake nodded grimly. "Can't be helped. All we can do is streak for Fort Bridger. You go first, then her, and I'll come last."

Ed urged the placid Mabel close to Spook. Iris's eager smile energized the frosty air between them, and Ed knew he would do anything in his power to make her safe and happy. She wrapped the

123

end of the muffler firmly around her face. All he could see now were her rich, dark eyes, her long eyelashes and deep brown eyebrows, where a fluffy snowflake landed, melting from the warmth of her skin.

Their situation was precarious, Ed knew, but it didn't seem to matter. Iris had summoned the courage she needed, and she was going with them. Nothing else could dim his elation. Not his cold toes and fingers, not the hostile rancher, not the driving snow.

He couldn't help smiling back at her. "Ready to enter Wyoming Territory, Miss Perkins?"

Chapter 23

Darkness fell, and Laura sat by the stove, listening and hoping. There was no sound but the soft sigh of the wind as it sifted the snow around the little house. The storm had continued all day, and a good eighteen inches of fresh snow stood in sheltered places. In the open, it drifted and blew. In some spots, the bleached grass poked through defiantly, but in others four-foot drifts collected.

On her return from the fort, she had run Shakespeare and the four horses from the corral into the barn with the Thoroughbred mare they'd caught and her foal, and she knew they were safe, if cramped. Jake had laid up a modest supply of hay and oats, counting on some open grazing during the winter. The scouring winds blew through the valley most years, he told her, and opened places where animals could find sustenance. It made the place a refuge for herds of deer and elk, and in recent years for emigrants' cattle.

She had gone over and over the trail in her mind, picturing each landmark, the rocks and spires, and the old fortifications built by the Mormons a few years back. If they traveled fast and met no mishaps, Jake and his brother might get to Zale's and be back tonight. Their trip a few days earlier had been slow as they canvassed homestead after homestead, searching for animals to buy. Leading those they purchased had hampered their progress as well. But a quick, direct run to Zale's and back would not take so very long.

All day she watched the snow fall, hating the early storm, willing it to abate. When she saw that it would not happen, she pleaded with God to protect Jake and Ed.

"Just bring them home safe, Father. That horse is not important."

If Jake wasn't home by daylight she would somehow make her way back to the fort and beg her father to send his men out immediately, blizzard or no blizzard.

She took the family Bible down and opened it resolutely, hoping to find comfort once more in the Psalms. *Why art thou cast down, O my soul? And why art thou disquieted within me? Hope thou in God; for I shall yet praise him for the help of his countenance.*

She closed her eyes and spoke silent words of praise, resting her fingertips on the printed words. Her panic faded, and her faith resumed its rightful place in her heart. God was in control, and Jake was safe in His hand.

She saw once more Iris Perkins' troubled face as she hid the New Testament in her gathering basket. "Lord, help Iris to find comfort in you, too. Show her your strength and your love."

It was very late when the wind died. Laura jerked awake. She had fallen asleep in Jake's mother's bentwood rocker. She loved the graceful chair that his father had carried up the steep places in the trail so long ago, so the woman he loved would have a comfortable seat in their new home. She stretched and shivered. The fire was low. She must have slept for some time.

Slowly she raked up the coals and filled the firebox with dry wood.

She hoped Jake and Ed were snug in the loft of the Glucks' house. She wouldn't allow herself to form a mental picture of them huddled over a campfire in the snow. Or worse.

I should have told him, she thought. She seemed to have a habit of putting off sharing important news. This time she'd waited too long.

She had thought he wouldn't let her go on their trip into Utah if he knew. He wouldn't want her to rough it, sleeping on the cold ground in the chilly autumn. He was a man who planned carefully, who looked for ways to cut the chances of calamity. Jacob Sherman was certainly not a man to take risks with the life of his first-born child.

126

But she hadn't been one hundred percent sure. She was hopeful two weeks ago, as they packed for the trip, but not certain. Now she knew. But she hadn't told him. She had planned to tell him when they were safely back again, and they would celebrate together in their home.

"Lord, I need him."

She wished she had told Jake, so that wherever he was tonight, he would know and have one more reason to fight whatever obstacles he encountered, and to come home.

Chapter 24

Ed pulled Mabel to a stop and waited for Spook to come alongside. Darkness had fallen early, and the fine, hard crystals of snow fell unremittingly. At least the blowing snow would obliterate their tracks quickly.

"I think the wind's letting up," he yelled.

Iris nodded and lifted one hand slightly, signifying that she heard and agreed. Ed turned to look over his shoulder, and saw that Jake was right behind them.

"It's not far."

Iris nodded again, and Ed urged Mabel forward. The horses plodded on, heads down. They'd earned a big ration and a peaceful night in a warm barn, Ed knew, but there was still work to be done. This day was the toughest one he'd ever spent on the trail, fighting the cruel elements.

They were only a couple of miles from the Sherman ranch when he heard a faint shout and turned back. Jake spurred Blaze up even with Spook, and the stallion stood with his sides heaving. Spook and Mabel huddled in toward him. Spook couldn't resist nipping at the sorrel's jaw, in a perfunctory attempt to redress past wrongs. Blaze squealed half-heartedly and tossed his head.

"He looks worn out," Ed shouted.

"Just about. He danced around so much the first hour, he's got no steam left. But I think we've got company."

Ed jerked upright and stared down the dark trail behind them.

"I thought I was hearing something before," Jake said, "but now I'm sure. Every time the wind slacks, I hear it."

"Zale?" Ed asked.

Iris stared at him, and even in the darkness he sensed her terror.

"Probably." Jake pulled off his left glove and blew on his fingers. "Best send Iris on ahead."

"What?" she wailed. "I don't know where we're going!"

Ed reached out and laid his aching fingers on her sleeve. He'd only kept his hands from freezing by alternating them on the reins and keeping the free one in his pocket. "Give Spook his head. He'll take you home."

Jake nodded. "It's less than two miles. He'll get you there, no matter what. Pound on the door. Tell my wife we're coming. She'll get you warm and tend the horse."

Iris pulled in a deep breath and stared at him. "What if you don't come?"

"We'll be there soon, but I want you out of sight. Tell Laura I said to hide you."

Ed had been straining to hear what Jake had detected. "They're coming. Jake's right, Iris. You go now, before they see you." He squeezed her arm slightly, and wondered if she could feel it.

She hesitated, and he looked at Jake.

"Go with her," Jake said.

Ed was torn. He wanted to be with Iris, to see her safely to Laura's door, but he didn't dare think what might happen to his brother if he raced on ahead with her.

"I'm not leaving you to face them alone," he said.

"I'll go." Iris sound terrified, and Ed placed his hand over hers briefly, then stroke Spook's neck.

"God will go with you." It was all he could offer her.

"Go fast," Jake said shortly. There was no mistaking the rapid hoofbeats now.

She looked at them in one last moment of desperation, then turned Spook up the trail and dug her heels in. The huge gray was a shadow in the night, and then he was gone.

"Do we ride?" Ed asked his brother.

"Best stand and wait for them. Give her time to get to the house."

Ed pulled his rifle out and sent up a quick prayer as he settled himself firmly in the saddle with a short rein.

Several riders rode around the bend in the trail at a trot, and the leader gave a whoop when he saw them.

"Steady, now," said Jake.

Ed gritted his teeth as half a dozen horses jogged up, snorting and panting, to surround them.

"Well, Sherman." Zale rode up to Jake, his horse facing Blaze. "I see you're riding my horse."

"My horse, sir," Jake said, sitting still. Blaze fidgeted, but Jake held him in check.

"Where's Iris?" A young man demanded shrilly.

"Hush, boy," Zale snarled.

Ed stared at the boy, but couldn't make out his features. Must be Zale's son, the oafish one who had laid claim to Iris.

"That horse was taken from my barn this morning," Zale said.

Jake met the large man's gaze evenly, his shoulders squared. "I'll not deny it, but he's not your horse, and you know it."

Ed was relieved to see that Zale was not riding the younger stallion, but was mounted on a sleek spotted gelding. Another man, whose beard was white, pushed his horse up next to Zale's.

"Do you have proof of ownership?"

"Yes, sir, I have a bill of sale signed by Isaac Zale."

"Well, then, just show it to me, if you please."

Jake hesitated, and Ed felt a surge of panic. He had seen his brother hand the bill of sale to Laura after they left Zale's ranch two days before, and she had placed it in the pocket of her green wool coat. How would these men react if Jake told them? His index finger slid toward the trigger of his rifle.

"It's not here," Jake said. "It's at home."

"Where's home?" The older man's tone implied that he was certain Jake was lying. Ed wondered what story Zale had told about them.

"Not more than two miles from here, sir. You're all welcome to come on and warm up, and I'll show you the paper."

Ed caught his breath. Was Jake crazy? He would expose Laura and Iris to these thugs. The six men could overpower them, take the paper and the horse, and force Iris to go back to Utah with them.

The young man called out, "Sounds good, Pa. We're gonna freeze to death if we sit here much longer."

Ed realized that, although the wind had lessened, the temperature was still well below freezing. It wouldn't do the horses or the men any good to prolong their outing.

Jake looked Zale in the eye. "You're all welcome to come and sleep by the fire, and we'll feed you breakfast before you head home."

The second man looked to Zale. "What do you say, Isaac? We can settle this thing in comfort."

Zale spat into the snow. "That horse goes home with me in the morning, Pilcher."

The other man said soothingly, "Certainly, if this man can't supply a bill of sale."

Jake said nothing, and Zale squinted at him.

"Where's the girl?"

"Girl?"

"Don't pretend you don't know what I'm talking about. You must have seen her when you came to my house."

"No, sir, I didn't."

"Well, she left this morning, and that horse left, too. He didn't saddle himself. And you didn't come out here on foot. Somewhere there's another horse, and I'll wager Iris Perkins is riding him."

"Let's head on to my ranch and discuss this over coffee," Jake said.

"No tricks."

"I'm not one to pull tricks," Jake said grimly.

"Pa, my toes are friz."

Zale turned to fix him with a glare. "Silence, Rufus."

The young man circled his horse but kept quiet.

"All right, Sherman," said Pilcher. "You lead the way. We're too far from home to go back tonight, and it's too cold to camp."

Jake nodded at him and turned Blaze homeward. He kept the pace steady and even, and Ed knew he was giving Iris more time.

Chapter 25

The wind howled around the drafty barracks at Fort Bridger, and Hal Coleman paced back and forth between the bunks restlessly. His main duty at the fort was caring for the remounts, and the horses were as snug as he and Riley, the Texan who shared his duties, could make them on a night like this. His thoughts were on the Sherman brothers, and he wished he knew if they'd made it safely back to Jake's ranch. He tried not to think of the alternatives, but then thoughts of home rushed in to replace his fretting about Jake and Edward.

It was more than three years since he had seen his wife and little daughter. He was counting the days until he could head back east, for Georgia and home. He'd planned to go a year ago, but Liza had written him that the crops had been poor and his parents were in dire straits. She had to use some of the pay he sent her to buy supplies for the family, so Hal had signed on for one more year. He hoped desperately that it was enough, and that his father was able to make a crop this year, or to find work that paid cash. But no matter, he was going home.

Captain Byington had told him a week ago that he could transfer to Fort Laramie the first of December. That would put him a week's ride closer to Liza and Molly when his enlistment expired at the end of the year.

He had no pictures of his loved ones. Photographers were rare where he came from. After he'd reached Independence on his way west to join the Sixth Cavalry, he'd had a daguerreotype made of him wearing his uniform and sent it back to Liza, but all he had to remember her by was a lock of her fine, dark hair.

He tried to imagine Molly at five years old, and couldn't. The girl was talking some when he left, toddling around and hanging on to Hal's pant leg. He had hauled her around on his back a lot, and tucked her into the trundle bed each night. Molly was a wonderful girl, and Hal looked forward to being with her again. She'd be big enough to take fishing now, and she'd have learned her letters, if Liza had time to teach her. With finances so tight she might be too busy to teach her the things she found laborious herself. Liza wasn't much of a reader to begin with.

He sent her every cent he could, but that wasn't much. The plan had been to put by enough for them to buy their own land when he mustered out, but letters from home told him that wasn't likely to happen soon. It was time he went home and took charge again. When it came down to it, he never should have left them. Enlisting was a big mistake, he could see that now. Even though the life on the plains still held a certain fascination for him, the ache in his heart whenever he thought about Liza and Molly outweighed that decisively.

He went to his bunk and lit the lantern that hung from the frame of the bed above his. There was nothing to do on long, cold evenings like this except crawl under the blankets and read. Jake had loaned him a book, and he pulled it from his rucksack. *Ivanhoe.* Laura said it was exciting. If that couldn't distract his thoughts from home and his friend's plight, probably nothing could.

He had just settled down when the door of the barracks opened suddenly, slamming back against the frame of the nearest bunk as the wind caught it. Captain Byington stood in the doorway, squinting in the irregular light. He fumbled for the door, and Markheim jumped to help him close it against the blast of frigid air.

The captain's appearance in the barracks was unprecedented, and all the men hastened to stand at attention. Hal climbed quickly out of his bunk.

"Coleman," the captain said, peering about the long room.

"Over here, sir."

"At ease, men." Byington quickly closed the distance between them. "Sorry to interrupt your leisure time, Coleman, but I'd like a word with you."

"Yes, sir." Hal pulled on his boots and reached for his coat.

When they were outside the barracks, there was no chance of conversation, as the wind tore at them and snatched away their breath. Byington leaned into it and plodded across the small parade ground toward his office, motioning for Coleman to follow.

"Sorry," he said again, gasping as he closed the door.

"That's all right, sir." It was suddenly very quiet and warm in the little room, and Hal saw that the heating stove was quite hot, as a coffee pot on top of it was pouring forth a steady plume of steam.

"I'm worried about my daughter," Byington began. "I know it's an awful night, but I think I'll ride out there."

Coleman eyed him cautiously. "Hard going, sir. It's five miles."

"I know it, but there's been no word, and I don't like to think of Laura all alone out there. Of course, Jake and his brother may have come in safely by now, but still ..."

"I'll go," Hal said quickly. It was unthinkable to let the captain start out in this storm alone. "You stay here, sir."

"No, then I'd just worry until you came back, and I wouldn't ask you to make a ten-mile round trip in this weather. I can stay with Laura until her husband gets back, or at least until morning. If he's not back then and the storm abates, I'll send you out with a detachment. I'm not waiting any longer than sunup. Just wanted to give you some warning, so you'll be ready."

"Sir, I think I'd better go with you." Hal could see there was no holding the captain down.

"I wouldn't ask that of you, Coleman. This is personal."

"I understand, sir, but it's personal for me, too. I've been thinking on it all day, wondering if I did right to leave those boys alone out there. Jake's the best friend I ever had. Anything could have happened. I should have risked discipline and stuck with them."

"No, you did the right thing."

137

Hal glanced toward the coffee pot. "Well, sir, it would probably be best to wait out the worst of this storm. It would be too easy to lose the trail in the dark and the snow. It's drifting something fierce."

Byington sighed and sank into the chair behind his desk. "You're probably right. I just don't like to think of Laura alone and frightened. She was afraid of the dark when she was little."

"She's all grown up now, sir, and if you don't mind me saying it, she's turned out solid. She'll be trusting in the Lord tonight."

Byington rubbed his hand across his eyes. "Of course you're right. Would you like some coffee?"

"No, thank you, sir. I'd best turn in if we're hitting the trail at first light."

"Yes." Byington started to stand up, then stopped as his glance fell on a leather bag on the edge of the desk.

"Say, you know those three men who came in this afternoon from Fort Laramie?"

"Yes, sir. I heard they were about done in. Their horses were near exhaustion when they were brought to the stable."

Byington nodded. "They were fortunate to make it in before the worst of the storm took hold. But I mentioned it because they brought mail with them."

Hal raised his eyebrows. There must be a reason the captain was telling him this, instead of letting the sergeant announce it at breakfast. Byington reached for the pouch and opened it, spilling two dozen envelopes onto the desk top.

"I'm sure I saw your name in here somewhere."

Hal stepped closer, trying not to show his eagerness.

Byington's hand closed on a letter. "There it is. From Georgia, unless I miss my guess." He smiled and held it out.

Hal swallowed and reached out slowly. "Thank you, sir."

"Sit down, sit down."

Hal hesitated.

"It's all right," Byington assured him. "If we're not going anywhere tonight, I need to bank this fire and get to bed. Take a minute and read it here in private."

"Thank you, sir."

Byington chuckled. "I had a letter from my older daughter, Elaine. Things are going well for her in Albany, and it seems I'll have a third grandchild before spring. I'll take the letter out to show Laura in the morning."

He picked up the poker and opened the door to the stove. Hal felt self-conscious as he sat down in an oak chair and tipped the envelope toward the kerosene lamp. He caught his breath. The handwriting was strange. Not Liza's, not his mother's or even his father's wobbly scrawl. It was a flowery but bold copperplate. He pulled his knife and slit the edge of the paper.

He sat in stunned silence, staring at the words. He began again at the top, but the news was no better than it had been the first time. A great rage began to grow in his heart, and his breath came quick and shallow.

Byington turned from the stove. "Well, now—" He stared at Hal. "Are you all right, Coleman?"

Hal looked at him, then toward the lamp. "I—no, sir—I—" He heaved himself to his feet. "I'll be ready at dawn, sir."

"Thank you."

Hal swung toward the door, but stopped with his hand on the iron latch when the captain spoke sharply.

"Wait!"

He turned slowly. "Yes, sir?"

"Coleman, I hope it's not—you don't look well."

Hal licked his lips and made himself meet the captain's eyes. "It's a blow, sir."

"I'm sorry. I thought it would be good news, or I—please forgive my insensitivity."

Hal nodded.

"If there's anything I can do …" Captain Byington's brow was furrowed in concern, and his brilliant blue eyes were troubled. Hal realized this man was more his mentor than his own father had ever been. He was a man who inspired loyalty in his subordinates. He worked hard, and he always checked up on things like supplies and rations, to be certain the men were as comfortable as possible at the austere outpost. He expected much from them, but also drove himself to set an example for them.

"It's Mrs. Coleman," Hal managed to say, in spite of the huge lump in his throat. He couldn't bear to say *Liza*. "My little girl, too. Typhoid." He felt tears forming in his eyes, but he didn't try to stop them.

Captain Byington sat down slowly. "I'm so sorry. I got a letter like that once myself."

Hal blinked hard and took a slow, deep breath. The entire scene had taken on a terrible unreality. The small, cramped office, the glowing lamp, the captain's gleaming buttons, the smell of the leftover coffee, and the wind howling outside made a dreamlike setting for his nightmare.

"Please excuse me, sir."

"Of course. And don't worry about me in the morning, Coleman. I can make it to the Shermans' on my own."

"No, sir. I'll have the horses ready at sunup. You'll want your new gray?"

"Yes, he's the strongest, but—"

"I'll be ready." Hal turned and opened the door, bracing himself against the cruel wind.

Chapter 26

Laura sat up, straining to hear. She'd turned out the lamp and sat up in her rocker by the fireplace, with only the firelight glowing softly. She hoped without real expectation that Jake would come back this evening. Now it was much later than her usual bedtime, and she had dozed off in her chair. Was it hoofbeats she had heard? The wind had dropped to an eerie moan, but there! There was a thud and a bump at the doorstep, then frantic pounding on the solid oak panel.

"Mrs. Sherman! Please hurry!"

The distraught voice startled Laura, and she rushed across the small room to throw the bar off its mounts. She knew instantly that the padded figure tumbling across the threshold into her arms was Iris.

"Come in child. What's happened? Are you alone?"

She scooted the girl toward her rocker, unwinding the ice-encrusted scarf from around Iris's neck as she spoke.

"It's brother Zale. We heard horses coming after us."

"After who? Iris, did you meet my husband?"

"Yes! Oh, Mrs. Sherman, I'm sorry, but I'm afraid I've caused a great deal of trouble for your family." Iris shivered as Laura eased her overcoat from her shoulders. The coat was nearly stiff with ice, and she tossed it on the floor, then bent to build up the fire.

"Sit down here, Iris. Warm up a bit, then tell me everything. I'll make you some tea."

"There's no time, Mrs. Sherman." Tears streamed down Iris's red, chapped face. "Your husband and his brother made me come on ahead, but Zale and his bunch were almost upon them. Isn't there anyone we can send to help them?"

Laura stood still with the poker in her hand. "No, there's no one. It's five miles to the fort."

"Mr. Sherman said you must hide me. I don't want to go back, but I don't want to cause trouble for you and your husband."

Laura thought quickly. "How far back were they when you left them?"

"Edward said two miles, but it seemed farther. I rode your horse in."

"Spook?"

"Yes! I'd have missed the trail a dozen times, but he knew where to go. He leaped right through the drifts."

"I must take care of him." Laura stepped briskly to the door and took her coat from a peg. "Sit down, Iris, while I go and put Spook in the barn."

Iris's eyes were large and dark with fear.

"Listen to me." Laura stepped closer as she folded a soft shawl about her head. "If you hear the men riding in, go in there and close the door. Do you understand?" She pointed toward the bedroom that had been Jake's parents', the one she and Jake had shared since their marriage.

Iris nodded silently and rubbed her arms, shivering. Laura took a precious moment to put another stick in the firebox of the small wood stove. Someday she'd have a fine kitchen range, but for now they made do with a box heater and were happy to have it. She pushed the teakettle onto the hottest part of the stovetop.

"I'll be back in five minutes. Get a blanket from my bed, child, and take off your boots if you can."

She dashed out into the cold. Spook jumped away from the step with a startled snort, then came back to her, nickering.

"Good old Spook! I should have brought you a treat!" Laura grasped the reins that trailed in the snow and led him quickly toward Jake's small, snug barn. It was full of horses already, but one more would just make them cozier on this frigid night. She turned him into the stall Jake had built extra strong for the stallion he had purposed to buy, since one of the new mares was at Spook's usual tie-up.

Jake had spread the floor thick with straw before their trip to Utah, in anticipation of bringing home a new occupant for the stall.

Laura went to the bin where he stored a week's worth of oats in the barn and half filled a bucket. When she took it to him, Spook plunged his nose eagerly into it.

"You need water, too, don't you, boy? I'll bring some warm from the house."

She made two trips, using nearly all the water she'd lugged in earlier, before Spook was satisfied. When she returned to the house at last, ready to attend to her guest, she found Iris sound asleep in the rocking chair with her damp, steaming coat pulled over her knees.

Laura set her stew kettle on the stove and added a little water. She fixed a cup of tea and put a biscuit and a piece of gingerbread on a plate, then carried them to the bedroom with a candle. After spreading back the bedclothes, she went back to the main room and nudged Iris's shoulder gently.

"Come, Iris. You need to lie down, dear."

Iris moaned and opened her eyes. She sat up suddenly, her face instantly vibrant with alarm. "Mrs. Sherman! What will we do? Your husband—"

"Hush now. Come and have some tea and lie down."

"But the men—"

"We'll leave it up to God." Laura took her hand and pulled Iris to her feet. "Come. I'll give you a nightdress. You must get out of those damp clothes."

Iris stared at her. "How can you be so calm?"

"Because God will do what is best."

Iris's forehead wrinkled. "Edward said God would go with me, and I think He's here now. Is He here with us, Mrs. Sherman?"

"He most certainly is." Laura guided Iris slowly toward the bedroom doorway.

"He's with you all the time, isn't he?" Iris stopped on the hooked rug and turned eagerly toward Laura. "Does the light of God shine in your heart?"

Laura smiled. "Sometimes that seems like the only light there is. Like now. Things look rather dark, don't they?"

"We are troubled on every side, yet not distressed," Iris said with wonder.

Laura's curiosity soared. "That's right. You said I was calm. I guess that's why."

"And we're not forsaken. That's in here, too." Iris tugged at the pocket of her skirt, forcing her hand through the layers of resistant wool, and pulled out the New Testament, bent and slightly bedraggled.

Laura smiled in understanding. "You've been reading it! I'm so glad."

"We are perplexed, but not in despair," Iris quoted. "I knew you would know what it all meant."

Laura hugged her, on the verge of tears. "I'd love to talk about it now, but you said Jake was coming, and it's been at least a quarter of an hour since you came. I've got to light the lamps and make coffee and half a dozen other things. You stay in here. Drink the tea and have a bite, then blow out the candle and rest."

She brought a soft flannel nightgown from her chest of drawers and closed the door on Iris. As she bustled about in the cozy front room Jake's father had built with loving hands, she prayed earnestly. Every time her thoughts strayed toward panic, she pulled herself up short and repeated the words Iris had said. *We are troubled on every side, yet not distressed.* Lord, show Iris your power. Let her understand your love and your goodness."

She had baked that afternoon, four loaves of bread, two pies, gingerbread, and dozens of oatmeal cookies, telling herself Jake and Ed would be ravenous when they came home. She had refused to let herself think, even for an instant, that they might never come home. As she began plundering the pantry, she caught a faint sound and ran to the front door.

The yard was full of horses, and one of them was the fiery stallion.

She wanted to shout Jake's name and run into his arms, but the deep voices of other men as they dismounted and headed for the

144

barn kept her back. Her heart pounding, she closed the door and dashed back to the pantry. She would need every scrap of food to feed this crew.

There were only six cups. The Shermans had been a family of six, and the pantry shelves held four tin cups and two ironstone mugs. She carried them all to the table, and the door rushed open.

"Miss me, darlin'?"

She laughed and flew to Jake, to be engulfed in his ardent embrace.

"Iris here?" he whispered in her ear.

"Yes."

"That's all right, then. But we've got company."

"I gathered that. How many?"

"Six, besides me and Ed."

"I've got tea and coffee and a few refreshments."

"Doughnuts?" he asked eagerly.

"No," she laughed. "Not this time. I'll make you some tomorrow. How does squash pie sound?"

Chapter 27

"This horse is soaking wet."

"What?" Ed turned to face the older man, Pilcher, in the dim lantern light. The barn was over-full now, but they couldn't leave the exhausted horses outside.

"This gray horse in the box stall. He's dripping with sweat."

Ed frowned. "Maybe he's got colic. I'd better tell Jake."

"Colic, my eye." Zale pushed past him, into the stall. "This is that big gray your sister-in-law was riding the other day."

Ed kicked himself mentally. Zale would notice a good horse.

"We'd better put the red stallion in here, or he'll kick up a ruckus with the other horses," he said.

But Zale was not distracted. "Someone's been riding this gelding hard."

"I expect you're right," said Ed. "It's Mrs. Sherman's horse, as you say, and she loves to ride. Are you gents ready for some coffee?"

Jake met them at the door of the little house. Laura and Iris were nowhere in evidence, but the table was covered with food—venison stew, fresh bread and butter, pies, cookies—and Jake immediately began pouring coffee. The box stove was glowing red on the side, and the fire in the fireplace had been replenished with dry wood.

"Sidle up to that fire, gentlemen," Jake called.

"My toes are friz right off," Rufus Zale whined.

"Hush," said his father.

"Take your boots off," Jake said genially. "If it's serious, I'll get you a pan of water to soak them in." Ed stared at him, and Jake grinned. He was the host now, and things were going his way for the

147

moment. "My wife outdid herself with baking today, and you all get to sample her delectable gingerbread and pie."

The men seemed less belligerent now that warmth and food were in the offing, and Ed sat down on a bench near the door, watching them uneasily. The room was overcrowded, and smells of hot wool and sweat soon overpowered the aromas of coffee and fresh bread.

Zale had claimed the rocker, and the other men lounged in kitchen chairs. Rufus Zale and another young man sat on a bench near the wood stove. They all looked large to Ed, and he tried to figure their odds in a fight. He didn't like it.

"Well, now," Pilcher said after a bowl of stew, two thick slices of bread and jam, and a piece of pie, "we ought to be able to settle this little dispute, Mr. Sherman. Let's have that bill of sale you mentioned."

"Well, sir," Jake said with a smile, somewhat strained, Ed thought, "it turns out the joke's on me. I thought the paper was here, but my wife tells me it's not."

"What do you mean?" Zale jumped up, sending the rocker slamming back against the log wall.

"Take it easy," Pilcher murmured.

"I mean that it's not here," Jake said evenly. "When the horse escaped yesterday and I took off after him, my wife went to Fort Bridger and left the bill of sale in the safekeeping of Captain Byington."

Glances passed between the Mormon men.

"That seems a bit unusual," Pilcher said. His beard was nearly white, and the others seemed to respect him and let him speak for them.

"Not really," said Jake. "You see, the captain is my father-in-law."

Pilcher tipped his chair back. "I see."

Zale took a step toward Jake. "Look, he's lying. There never was a bill of sale. He saw the horse and liked it, and he came back this morning and stole it."

"And what does the Perkins girl have to do with all this?" Pilcher asked thoughtfully.

"How should I know? Maybe they kidnapped her."

"Gentlemen," Jake said stiffly, "I think we all need some sleep. There's a loft yonder with two bunks, where some of you can bed down. The rest can sleep on the floor up there, or here near the fire. Edward, you take your sister's old room. In the morning we can all ride to the fort and see Captain Byington and end this thing."

Ed's brain whirred. He was so tired he couldn't think straight. But where was Iris? Surely Laura didn't have her stashed in one of the outbuildings or the root cellar. But Jake had offered him Vivian's old bedroom, so she couldn't be in there.

Jake piled the dishes on the work table where Laura's dishpan sat. "There's some blankets in the loft," he went on. "If any of you brought bedrolls, that will help. I've got a few horse blankets in the barn, if you need 'em."

"I'm thinking one of us ought to sleep in the barn," Zale said slowly.

Jake shrugged. "If you want to freeze, it's up to you." He nodded amicably. "Good night, gentlemen. Ed."

To Ed's chagrin, his brother opened the door to his parents' bedroom—Jake and Laura's room now—and disappeared, closing it firmly.

~~~~~

Laura stepped back from the door when she heard Jake approaching. She'd been listening, her heart pounding, as the men talked.

As soon as he had shut the door, she had her arms around him. He pulled her close in the darkness and leaned back against the door.

"It's all right. We'll settle things tomorrow. Sorry I had to turn this place into an inn, but I couldn't send them out again. It's mighty cold."

"I don't care, as long as you're here."

Jake chuckled and kissed her. "Well, I can't stay here exactly. Iris asleep?"

"Yes, poor thing. Jake, she's been reading my Bible."

"Praise God. Let me hook the latch." She heard him slide the hook into place. "Keep that door locked. Don't you go out of this room in the morning until I tell you to."

"All right."

Jake walked softly across the room to the window. "Poor Edward. I'll probably scare the daylights out of him. See you in the morning, sweetheart. You're a good sport."

"Jake—"

He had the window open and was halfway out.

"What is it?"

"Nothing. Go on. It's cold."

He leaned toward her and brushed her lips briefly with his. "When this crowd clears out tomorrow, we'll catch up, you and me." He slid over the windowsill, and Laura watched him creep along the wall to Ed's window, then closed the shutter. It didn't seem right, sending her husband out by way of the window. She took off her shoes and lay down beside Iris, burrowing in under the quilts. She was too nervous to undress, with six strange men in the house, but Iris seemed to be sleeping peacefully.

Chapter 28

Before dawn, Laura wakened. Iris was turning over, tugging gently at the quilt.

"Iris?"

"Mrs. Sherman?"

"Yes. Call me Laura."

"Are they gone?"

"No. They're all sleeping out in the front room, or in the loft."

"Do they know I'm here?"

"No. But they suspect."

"Brother Zale won't let your husband keep Red. I know he won't. Somehow, he'll get him back."

Laura shivered. "There's one man who seems reasonable, even if he doesn't believe Jake entirely. I think his name is Pilcher."

"He's an elder."

"Is he fair?"

"I don't know."

"Well, Jake said to stay in here until he tells me to go out and get breakfast."

"Can I help you?"

"No. Those men would see you. You'll have to stay in here. They plan to ride to the fort and see my father this morning. After they all leave, you can come out and eat something."

"All right." Iris was quiet for a moment. "I'm sorry to have disrupted your family."

"It's not your fault. There would have been a scene over the horse, anyway."

"Yes, but—well, if I weren't here, you could have had time to talk to your husband. Is he all right?"

"Yes, he and Edward are fine." Laura smiled to herself. "There was something I wanted to tell him, but it will wait."

"I knew I was in the way."

"No, it's nothing. Well, it's something, but ..."

"Is it a baby?"

Laura gasped. "How did you know?"

Iris sat up. "I don't know. It just came into my head that it would be something special you wanted to tell him."

Laura lay back on the pillow, grinning in the darkness. "Yes, it's very special."

"Aren't you scared?"

"No, why would I be? I'm very excited about it. Jake will be absolutely wild."

"But what if ..."

"I don't allow what-if's," Laura said. "The Psalm says *Wait on the Lord, be of good courage.* That's what I try to do. And God does the rest."

Iris's voice was so low Laura could barely hear her. "Do you really like being a wife?"

"It's the best thing that ever happened to me." Laura reached out and clasped Iris's hand. "Of course, the Lord gave me a wonderful husband."

"I read those places that said an elder of the church is to have one wife. I guess you know they don't think that way."

"That's not the only requirement," Laura said. She knew who Iris meant by *they.* "They're supposed to be sober-minded, too, and hospitable—"

"Your Jake is more hospitable than Brother Zale."

"And all husbands are to love their wives."

"Yes." Dawn was approaching, and Laura could see Iris now. She was watching her pensively. "Could you tell me about the rest of it now, Mrs.—Laura?"

"The rest of what, dear?"

"There's more to it, I know. How does God's light shine in your heart? Because I want it in mine. More than anything else, I want that."

~~~~~

Jake and Ed rose early. After a brief conference with his brother, Jake crawled out the window and in through Laura's.

"Ed and I will go feed the horses. You can get dressed and start breakfast."

"I'm dressed." Laura threw back the quits and sat up on the edge of the bed, with a rueful smile toward Iris, who was still huddled beneath the covers. "I guess I wasn't as calm as I let on last night."

"Slept in your clothes?" Jake smiled and kissed her. "That shows me you're human."

He glanced toward Iris and found she was watching them wide-eyed.

"Beg your pardon, ma'am. I'll get out of here."

He went out into the front room with Laura, and Ed joined him to tote water and firewood, then go to the barn to tend the horses. Isaac Zale had beaten them to it. He was in the stall with Blaze, running his hands down the stallion's legs.

"Everything satisfactory, Mr. Zale?" Jake asked, leaning on the divider.

"Hmpf." Zale straightened.

"Sir, I don't know why you're making this fuss, but we can settle it mighty fast if you admit to your friends that you sold me this horse. I paid you good money, and you know it."

Zale's eyes narrowed. "I know no such thing."

Ed stepped up beside his brother, unable to contain his fury. "You hoped you could catch up with us and get Blaze back however you could. Well, your friend Pilcher seems to have a little bit of sense and integrity, unlike yourself. Just go home, Zale."

Zale's face colored. He leaned toward Ed and said slowly, "Listen to me, boy, that horse goes back to Zion, one way or another."

Ed looked at Jake uneasily. What if they never made it to the fort? What if Zale and the others attacked them here at the ranch?

~~~~~

Laura worked quickly, measuring out the coffee and stirring up a triple batch of griddle cakes. She wished Jake would come back. The bearded men had roused, and two of them sat on the bench, watching her every move. She set a skillet on the stove for bacon. This unexpected invasion was going to seriously deplete their larder.

A young man came down the ladder from the loft, and she immediately pegged him as Rufus Zale. She had seen him only from a distance at his home, but he had the same eyes, the same broad shoulders and stocky build as his father. His thin red beard was short and patchy. He stared at her, and that, too, was like his father. She shuddered and turned her back.

Zale came in from outside and rallied the men to gather their things and eat quickly. He personally wolfed down an enormous stack of pancakes and a half pound of bacon. "The weather's cleared. We'll humor this fellow by riding over to the fort, I guess. Then we head for home."

Pilcher and one of the other men approached her deferentially as the rest poured through the door.

"Thank you, Mrs. Sherman," said Pilcher. "You've been most gracious. This cannot have been easy for you."

"Don't mention it." She couldn't force a smile. "I'm praying you will be fair in this, Mr. Pilcher."

"A misunderstanding," he said smoothly. "If your husband shows us the receipt, then—"

"*If*," Laura cried. "You're calling me a liar, sir. I personally took that bill of sale to the fort. You're implying that I'm lying."

Pilcher backed away. "I'm sorry, ma'am. I didn't intend to insult you."

The other man looked down at the floor. "Thanks for the eats, ma'am."

She took a deep breath. "You're welcome."

There was a bustling and shouting outside, and the two men went out to join the others. Laura waited a moment, then went to the bedroom door.

Iris jumped up from the edge of the bed. "What's happening? I'm going crazy in here!"

"They're leaving. Just sit still for a few more minutes, and they'll be gone."

"Did they ask about me?"

"Nothing more was said about you this morning. Perhaps they'll let it go."

Iris shook her head. "Not Brother Zale. He's got something up his sleeve."

Chapter 29

Ed saw Laura come to the door of the house. The blue shawl she had wrapped around her emphasized the vivid color of her eyes, and the cold sunlight glinted off her honey-gold hair. His brother was doubly blessed, Ed thought, with a woman both intelligent and beautiful.

A sudden longing to see Iris hit him. If he and Jake did make it to Fort Bridger, he might not be allowed to leave again for days, even weeks. He couldn't just ride off and leave Iris now without speaking to her again. There was an intangible bond between them. He had felt it yesterday, as they'd struggled through the storm together. She must be anxious, not knowing what was happening. Was she thinking of him? He needed to let her know that he cared about her and would still be thinking of her, even if he couldn't come back to see her for a while.

Zale had insisted Jake bring the peppery stallion along to the fort, so that he wouldn't have to return to the ranch if his claim were upheld, and Jake was busy saddling Blaze. Ed ambled toward Laura and looked around. No one seemed to be paying attention to him.

"Everything all right?" he asked.

She nodded.

He leaned close to her ear. "Can I see her?"

Laura's brilliant eyes flared. "Not now, Edward. It's too dangerous."

"I—I just want to see her for a minute. I may not be able to come back later, once I've reported in at the fort."

"Well…"

He could see that Laura was wavering. She had a romantic streak as wide as Wyoming, he knew that. "Remember how it was you first fell in love with Jake?" he whispered.

She closed her eyes for a moment, then sighed. "All right, but be careful."

He smiled, and she stepped aside for him to enter.

He crossed the front room quickly and tapped on the bedroom door. There was no response.

"Iris?" he asked softly. "It's me, Edward."

He heard a soft metallic chink, then the door opened just a crack. He smiled involuntarily as one of her violet eyes peered out at him cautiously.

"Is it safe?"

"They're still in the dooryard. I wanted to see you."

"Why?"

That threw him for a second. "I guess—well, I just wanted to."

"You're going to the fort with them?"

"Yes, I need to get back, and anyway, I don't want Jake to go alone. I don't trust them."

"You shouldn't. I'm surprised they didn't pull something already. Maybe they're not all bad, but those Zales are not ones you want to turn your back on."

"I'll keep that in mind."

She opened the door a few more inches, and they stood silent for a long moment. He realized he was staring at her. It was the first time he'd seen her in full daylight without her heavy wraps. She wore the functional Bloomer costume that many of the Mormon women wore on the windy plains. It was a deep, lavender gray that suited her, bringing out the tint in her eyes. Her hair flowed over her shoulders in a dark cascade, and her tanned cheeks were smooth and flawless. Her look held a deep determination and a passionate hope he hadn't expected.

Suddenly a blush colored her face, and she turned away. "I should have put my hair up, but I didn't like to use Laura's things without asking her."

Ed took a step toward her. "Don't go back with them, Iris."

She kept her back to him, and her voice cracked a little as she said, "I don't want to. Laura thinks your brother can make them leave me alone."

"If Jake and I have anything to say about it, you'll stay here."

She half turned then, and he caught his breath. She was not as beautiful as Laura, but her serious, sweet face, and her courage, combined with her wistful vulnerability, fanned his attraction to her.

"Laura says we're sisters in Christ now." She said it shyly, glancing up at him from beneath her dark lashes, then away.

Ed swallowed. It was more than he had hoped for, so soon. He reached out to touch her shoulder gently. "That's wonderful. I—I want you to stay. I'll do anything—Jake and I will—to see that you can."

"My father left me in the elders' care. If they find out I'm here—"

"They're not sure. We're taking them to the fort. Jake was worried at first, when he found out Laura gave the bill of sale to the captain, but it's turning out for the best. We'll get them away from here, so they won't have a chance of finding you."

"Thank you." She darted a glance up at him again, and his heart pounded.

"Iris—"

Her wide violet eyes were solemn, but she didn't flinch from his gaze this time.

"I do want to stay," she whispered.

Edward drew her toward him, his gaze holding hers. She cared for him, it was obvious. She wanted to stay here to be near him, not just because Laura had befriended her. He slid his fingers into her flowing hair. "Iris, if you don't see me for a few days, don't worry. As soon as I can, I'll come back. If you knew where your father was …"

"What?" Her lower lip trembled.

"I'd ask him if I could court you."

The long lashes hid her eyes. "What about the elders?"

"He didn't tell them they could marry you off like that, did he?"

"No, I don't think so. He told me he'd be back at the end of the summer, but it's been months now, and I don't even know if he's alive."

Ed drew a deep breath. He was standing on the edge of a precipice. If he didn't step back now, he never could. "I'd like to take care of you, Iris." He leaned down and kissed her gently. When he drew back, she stared up at him, her eyes wide. Then she smiled. Ed's stomach lurched, and he slid his arms around her.

The door crashed open.

"I knew it!"

They jumped apart, and Ed whirled to face Rufus Zale.

"I just knew you had her in here," Rufus crowed. "Pa!"

Ed grabbed him by the collar as he made for the door. "Stop!"

"Rufus," Iris pleaded, coming around to look him in the eye, "Please don't tell them! I've decided to leave Deseret. You'll only cause trouble if you tell them."

"You can't just up and leave without permission," Rufus sneered.

"Yes, she can," Ed said. He was dangerously close to losing his temper, and he took a deep breath. "Iris is old enough to make her own decisions, and she doesn't want to marry a scoundrel."

Rufus looked boldly at Iris. "You're promised to me, girl. Ain't no other man going to have you."

Ed pushed him against the door jamb between the rooms and held him there, applying pressure to his breastbone. "Don't say another word."

Fear flickered in Rufus's eyes. "We got a lot of men here, Sherman. We can stand you off in self-defense, you know."

Iris drew herself tall. "Go tell your father if you want to, but I'm never going back. I despise you, and I will never marry you."

Rufus glared at her. "You ought to be whipped. Maybe you will be."

Iris blinked and took a deep breath. Ed felt her turmoil.

"Please, Rufus." Her tone had softened, and Ed was confused, but he held Rufus, waiting to see what she would say. She came closer and looked earnestly at young Zale. "You know what it's like to want your freedom. I've seen you chafing against your father's strictness. Can't you understand? I know you'd rather be out on your own, have your own place. Your older brother has his own ranch now. But your father's keeping you at home to help him. He's profiting from your labor, Rufus. You aren't. You can understand what a hard man he is. If you want to stay under his thumb, fine, but don't force me into it, too."

Rufus hesitated, and Ed relaxed his grip just a little. "Let her stay," he said softly.

Rufus looked at him, and his eyes hardened. He jerked away suddenly and ran for the door. He was out of the house before Ed could catch him.

"Well, I guess we're in for it now," Iris said.

Ed stood irresolutely, looking after him. He turned to face her. "Are you all right?"

She gulped, and he saw that she was crying. "They'll take me away, Edward."

"No! I won't let them."

"Don't say that. No one defies Brother Zale without consequences."

Ed took a deep breath and stroked her cheek. "I'm sorry. I was careless, and this is my fault. I should have waited and spoken to you when it was safe. But whatever happens, I meant what I said." She came willingly into his arms, and his heart soared. "I want to take care of you, always, Iris. I want—"

The front door crashed against the wall, but he didn't jump away from her this time. He stood holding her as Isaac Zale stormed into the main room, his face a mask of fury.

"Take your hands off that girl!"

Ed turned slowly. Jake, Rufus, and Pilcher followed Zale into the house, and Laura trailed behind them.

Jake shook his head as if in disbelief that his brother had been so incompetent in keeping their secret. Rufus was smiling grimly, and Pilcher wore a puzzled air.

Laura marched past them to Iris. "Come on." She pulled Iris unceremoniously into the bedroom and shut the door. Ed squared his shoulders and turned to face the barrel of Zale's revolver.

~~~~~

Laura held Iris and let her weep on her shoulder.

"It's all right. Don't cry. It's going to work out."

"I'm sorry!" Iris dabbed at her eyes with her sleeve, and Laura stepped to the dresser and got her a handkerchief.

"Here. It's not your fault."

"I shouldn't have let him kiss me."

Laura stopped in her tracks. "Ed kissed you?" She hadn't thought he was ready to commit himself to Iris. It seemed foolhardy, in light of their short acquaintance, and with the hostile men still on the premises, but she was glad anyway. Jake had proposed to her within two weeks of their meeting, and neither had had any doubts that it was in God's plan. "Did you tell him?"

"Tell him what?"

"That you believe in Jesus as your savior?"

"I guess I did." Iris was laughing and crying at the same time.

Laura hugged her again. "I shouldn't have let him come to you, but he was so pathetic. It's going to be all right. I know it. Come, let's pray about this."

Through the door came Isaac Zale's angry voice. "That woman is betrothed to my son!"

Laura recognized Jake's even tones as he tried to soothe the older man, but she couldn't make out his words. She latched the bedroom door and pulled Iris down beside her on the edge of the bed. "This is one the Lord will have to sort out."

Iris's eyes were red-rimmed and full of fear. "What it they hurt Ed and Mr. Sherman? Laura, I'm so frightened."

Laura swallowed, trying to keep her own fear at bay. "God promises to protect his children, but even if something bad happens, he will sustain us."

"I can't bear it if they—"

There were shouts from the dooryard, and trampling footsteps as the men rushed outside.

Iris jumped up. "What's happening?"

Laura crossed quickly to the door and lifted the hook, peering out through a narrow opening. "I can't tell, but they left the front door open."

"If they're hurting Edward—"

A gunshot cracked, and there was sudden silence.

Chapter 30

"Stay here!" Laura ran across the front room and looked cautiously out the doorway. Ed and Pilcher, in an unlikely alliance, were wrestling Rufus Zale to the ground, and Jake lay in a heap near the corral gate. The other men were mounted and trying to control their skittish horses, except Isaac Zale, who stood on the ground holding Blaze's reins while the stallion plunged and reared. All of the horses snorted and pawed, circling restlessly and churning up the snow.

As Laura ran to her husband, Jake sat up slowly and looked around, fixing his gaze on Blaze with disgust.

"Whoa, now, Red," Zale commanded, but the stallion continued to pull at the reins and neighed shrilly.

"Jake, what happened? Are you all right?"

Jake sighed and struggled to his feet, wincing and holding on to the corral fence with his right hand. "The men out here hollered that the cavalry was coming, and we all ran outside to see. They were all mounting up, and Blaze was going crazy, so I tried to hold onto him, but then that fool Rufus fired his gun off."

Laura looked over to where Ed was jerking Rufus to his feet. The gleam in Ed's eyes told her he found some satisfaction in having an excuse to handle the young man roughly.

"You idiot!" Pilcher howled at Rufus. "They're not attacking us! You want to get us all killed?"

Blaze hopped away, using every new sound as an excuse to shy, but Isaac Zale held the reins firmly and got his arm under the stallion's chin, clamping his hand solidly on the sorrel's nose. "Whoa, you! Stand still, mister!"

Jake took a deep breath and rubbed the back of his head. "Must have hit on the fence post. Looks like your father's coming to call, sweetheart."

Laura whipped around and looked toward the trail that led to the fort. Two horsemen had stopped a hundred yards away, and were waiting with rifles drawn.

"Isn't that Father and Hal Coleman?"

"I'd say so, and I was never so glad to see anyone in my life."

Laura looked at him quickly. "Jake, you're hurt."

"Not much." He was holding his left wrist now, and Laura saw that his hand was swelling.

"Come inside." Zale seemed to have Blaze under control, and she turned toward Edward and Pilcher. "If any of you buffoons fires on Captain Byington again, you'll regret it. Edward, can you possibly bring some order here, while I tend to my husband?"

She turned to Jake again, and he grinned at her. He glanced around at the sheepish men and added, "Trust me, you don't want to tangle with Mrs. Sherman."

~~~~~

Iris waited in the corner near the fireplace while Laura and her father looked at Jake's injury. She refused to be banished again to the bedroom. The captain's presence had changed the atmosphere, and she felt safe for the moment. The Mormon men were waiting in the door yard, and Trooper Coleman stood near the window, keeping an eye on things. Ed sat on one of the benches watching his brother. When she looked his way, Ed gave her a wistful half smile. It warmed her, and she felt more confident, even though her future was unsettled.

"Looks like your wrist is broken, Jake. I'm sorry." The captain shook his head. "Most unfortunate."

"I'll live," Jake said. "Comfrey, that's what the Indians use for broken bones, and willow bark tea for pain."

He held still while Laura applied a snowball wrapped in a linen towel to his wrist.

"Tell me what the comfrey looks like, and I'll make the tea." Jake flinched at her touch, and she gritted her teeth. "Sorry."

"There's a man at the fort who can tend it for you," Byington said. "He's not a doctor exactly, but he apprenticed for surgery before he joined the army."

"Why didn't he become a doctor?" Laura asked.

Her father shrugged. "The scuttlebutt is, he had a drinking problem. I'll admit I've seen some evidence of it, but most of the time he's all right."

"He'll be sober this morning," Hal said.

"He'd better be."

"Just mash up some of those leaves in the little crock, Mrs. Sherman," Jake said dryly. "I'd rather take advice from a sober Indian than a soused trooper."

Laura went to the cupboard near her work table and took down a small earthenware crock.

"Let me help you." Iris left her spot in the corner. At least she could help her hostess now. "We call this boneset. It really does help."

"What do I do?" Laura asked.

"Brew the leaves and bind them over the wound. If you have the roots, they're good, too."

"I don't think we do." Laura frowned in concentration as she put a handful of the dried leaves in a stoneware bowl. "This is all stuff Jake or his mother gathered. He's teaching me, but I have no idea what this plant looks like when it's growing."

The captain turned his attention back to Jake. "Now, what's going on here? Your brother reported to me, but I don't see what all the wrangling is about. You bought a horse, and now the seller claims it's still his?"

"Yes, sir. Laura said she took the bill of sale to you, and I told these *gentlemen* I'd ride to the fort with them, so they could see it. I don't mind telling you I'll be glad to have you and Hal along. It evens the odds a bit."

"Of course," Byington said. "I've got the document in my safe. But how is the girl mixed up in this?"

Iris cringed as the captain's glance found her.

"I told you about Iris, Father," Laura said. She left her task, and Iris took over, putting a splash of hot water in the bowl and mashing the leaves into a pulp.

"She's the one who warned us there might be trouble when Jake bought the horse," Laura said. "Blaze escaped and went back to the Zales' ranch, and Iris rode him out to meet Jake, to return him. Those men came after her, and now Mr. Zale is claiming Jake and Edward stole the horse and kidnapped Iris."

"Kidnapped? That's a serious charge." The captain frowned at Jake and his brother.

"It's silly," Laura said. "She wants to leave Utah, and they won't let her. She's being forced into a marriage she doesn't want."

Byington looked her way again, and Iris wished she could shrink into the log wall.

"How old is she?" The captain asked softly.

"She's nineteen."

"I don't see a problem."

"Well, me either, and if she wants to marry Edward instead of Mr. Zale—"

"Whoa, there!" Byington's eyebrows arched as he surveyed his daughter. "Edward Sherman wants to marry this girl?"

"Woman, Father. She's a woman. You said so yourself. And, yes, my brother-in-law wants to court Iris. Can you blame him?" She threw Iris a sweet smile, and Iris lowered her gaze, feeling the blood rush into her cheeks.

Captain Byington looked at Edward, who had remained silent, but was blushing furiously. "Well, Private Sherman?"

"Yes, sir." Ed straightened automatically as the officer scrutinized him. He stood up. "If Miss Perkins will have me, it would be my pleasure to court her."

The captain nodded.

Laura glanced apologetically at Iris, and her face crinkled in remorse" It's my fault they know she's here. We hid her all night, but I let Ed come in to see her this morning, and they found out. I'm sorry, Iris. I knew better, and I should have insisted that he wait until he got back from Fort Bridger."

Iris was embarrassed by Laura's contrition for her error in judgment. It was as much her own fault. She ought to have sent Ed away immediately when he came to the door, but she'd been too thrilled to see him again. She'd wanted to hear the precious words he'd come to speak, to know that his feelings for her went beyond a simple desire to help someone in trouble.

She dumped the soggy leaves onto a clean dishcloth and folded it snugly. "Here's the poultice. Tie it onto Mr. Sherman's arm."

The captain walked slowly toward her. "Miss Perkins, I'm pleased to meet you."

"Sir." Iris made an abbreviated curtsey.

The captain seemed very thoughtful. "Have you promised yourself to this Zale man?"

She stared down at his gleaming black boots. "No, sir, it was not my choice."

"And how do you see your future, if you return to Deseret with these men?"

Anxiety washed over her as she thought about it. "I'd be married to Rufus Zale within a few days. I don't love him, and I shrink from the thought of marrying him."

"And on down the road, if you did?"

"Some would say I've no right to complain."

"How it that?"

"I'd be his first wife, sir."

"But you might not be his only wife."

"No. They say the elders are requiring—" She looked up at him quickly, wondering if she'd said something inexcusable. But Laura's father had a kind face, and his eyes were so unlike those of the Zale men that she took courage. "Sir, I don't believe their way anymore. I don't think it's right. I belong to God, and I don't think he'd have me marry one of the Saints. I want to leave them and learn more about the Bible. I know I'm supposed to obey the elders, but what they're asking of me doesn't seem right."

Captain Byington nodded thoughtfully.

Laura said as she wrapped Jake's wrist, "You don't have to obey those men, Iris. The Bible says women must obey their husbands, and their fathers if they don't have husbands, and maybe the government, but you don't have to obey anyone who tells you to do something against what God says."

"There's another consideration, sir," Jake said, wincing as Laura deftly knotted a strip of linen around his wrist, securing the poultice and makeshift bandage.

"And what is that?" Byington swung around to face his son-in-law.

"Rufus Zale threatened Iris, sir. My brother heard it."

Laura stamped her foot in anger, and her golden braid swung as she shook her head. "Father, you can't let them take Iris back."

"Settle down, Laura Margaret."

Iris almost laughed at Laura's spirited defense of her, but the knowledge that her future was in jeopardy took all the humor from the situation.

"Please, sir." Ed stepped forward, and Iris felt pride growing within her. "Laura can say what she will, but I know I'm the one who gave away Iris's presence, and I'm sorry about that. I intend to see that she's safe, and that she can choose her own future."

Captain Byington nodded. "All right, Sherman. But you have to understand, the federal government has an agreement with the Mormons. We can't interfere in their internal affairs."

"Father!" Laura's chin quivered and she scowled at him. "We are in Wyoming! They have no jurisdiction here!"

"True, Laura, but there are laws concerning—"

"Concerning fugitives and runaway slaves. Iris is neither. As an officer of the United States Army, it is your duty to protect this woman!" Laura fairly bristled at him, and the captain pressed his lips together. A fleeting glimmer of something like amusement crossed his rugged features. Jake turned away, but Iris saw his smile, and Edward just stared at Laura in awe.

The captain turned to Iris. "Miss Perkins, you are welcome to come to Fort Bridger for protection if you wish it. Of course, you may remain as my daughter's guest, if you prefer. Who knows? She may have a more effective arsenal than the U.S. Cavalry."

Laura launched herself at her father, engulfing him in a fervid embrace. "Thank you, Daddy! Thank you!"

Jake smiled and stood up, with just a slight grimace. "Well, now, I appreciate your help in all this, sir. What do you say we mosey over to the fort, wave a piece of paper under Zale's nose, and send these gents packing?"

Chapter 31

The temperature had climbed, and the snow was melting rapidly. The horses' breath no longer frosted in the air, and Jake thought they might just get a few more weeks of open weather before winter really set in. He hadn't waited around for the willow bark tea, and his left wrist ached terribly, but he would worry about that later.

He had switched horses with Hal, after realizing that Blaze's antics would continually send pain shooting through his arm. The stallion was still frisky, and Hal kept him on a tight rein next to Lady. When Blaze reached out to nip the mare's neck, Hal leaned over and clobbered the stallion's cheek.

"Leave my horse alone, you miserable flea bag! Honestly, Jake, I don't know why you bought this plug."

"Two days ago you thought he was a real find."

"That's before I knew about his manners, or lack of them."

Laura rode at the front of the column on Spook, at her father's side, and Ed came next on Shakespeare, while Iris rode beside him on docile Tramp. The Mormon contingent was behind them, with Jake and Hal bringing up the rear. Since the incident with Rufus, Pilcher seemed to be leaning toward the Shermans' side of the dispute, and Jake felt that the captain's presence guaranteed them safe conduct to Fort Bridger, but he still didn't feel comfortable enough to let the Zales ride behind him.

"Your brother and Miss Perkins seem to be getting along famously," Hal said.

Jake looked ahead and saw Ed leaning toward the girl and speaking to her nonstop, in a confidential tone. Iris's face was animated in response.

Jake shook his head. "Never saw a man fall so hard so fast."

Hal laughed. "What about you? You were just about out of your mind in love with Laura."

"Still am." Jake smiled at him. "Did I act that foolish?"

"Worse. But I don't know as Edward's being foolish. She seems like a real nice girl. Got into a bad fix, but it wasn't her fault, near as I can tell."

"Well, yes, but I hate to see him tie up too quick to someone with cumbersome baggage, if you take my meaning." Jake nodded toward the Zales. At that moment, Isaac Zale looked over his shoulder at him. His face was dark as a thundercloud. His son was riding behind him and his friends, in disgrace, his head hanging low.

Hal nodded and lowered his voice. "Pilcher says if you show him the bill of sale, they'll leave with no more questions. But if you can't . . ."

"I heard him. Blaze and Miss Perkins go back with them. Well, that's not going to happen. The captain's rock solid, and he's got the bill of sale. No problem."

Hal nodded. "So, then the way is open for Edward to pay his addresses to Miss Perkins. Ed's grown up a lot this year. He'll be all right."

"What about you?" Jake stood in the stirrups and stretched a little. "Better come for supper before you head for Laramie next week."

Hal looked off toward the Black Fork River, where it wound close to the trail. It would freeze up for the winter soon, but it still burbled merrily today.

"Well, there might be a change of plans."

"What for?" Jake watched his friend cautiously, but Hal wouldn't meet his eyes. He seemed ill at ease, and it wasn't due to Blaze's misbehavior.

"I got word last night that Liza and Molly are gone."

"Gone?"

"Typhoid went through Treat Valley in August."

"You mean—" Jake broke off, hovering between disbelief and outrage. A deep sorrow settled on him, and he saw from Hal's face that there was no mistaking his meaning. "I'm sorry."

Hal shrugged. "Hardly seems fair. You don't have to tell me God knows what He's doing. I know that. But it's hard to take."

Jake nodded. "What are you going to do?"

Hal sighed. "Don't rightly know. The captain and I talked some on the way out to your place. He said if I want to re-up, he'll recommend me for a promotion. Maybe get me on the Oregon Escort duty next summer."

"Do you want that?"

"I don't know what I want." Hal gave a short laugh that sounded more like a sob. "It's just not sunk in yet, I think."

"You should take some time to think about things before you make a decision. You might want to go back to Georgia. Your folks are still there."

Hal reached into his inner pocket and produced a letter. "I think I'd like you to see this. Tell me what you think." He unfolded the message and handed it to him.

Jake held the paper gingerly in his swollen hand and pored over it as Lady walked steadily along.

Dear Mr. Coleman, It is with great regret that I put pen to paper on this occasion, to inform you that your wife succumbed last evening to typhoid fever, and also the little girl. Your father is very feeble at present, and I have little hope for his recovery. Your mother and your cousin, Mrs. Snyder, have managed to avoid the sickness thus far. The community is in dire straits as many are ill, and I must hasten on to where I can help others in need. With deepest sympathy, Dr. George Harkins.

"Sounds like your daddy's bad off, too."

"That was written almost three months ago. He's likely gone now, too." Hal shook his head. "I hate being so far from them. Liza

175

and Molly are long buried, and I'm just finding out. All these months, I've been planning ..."

Blaze turned his head to nip at Lady again, and Jake kicked at his jaw with the toe of his boot. "Cut it out!"

Blaze lunged away, and it took Hal several seconds to regain control of the horse.

"Sorry," Jake said. "You've got enough to think about."

"I was so looking forward to seeing how big Molly had got," Hal said.

"You might write to your mother and wait to see what she says."

Hal reached for the letter. "I likely wouldn't get an answer for six months."

"Who's this Mrs. Snyder?"

"Oh, that's my cousin Ruby. Don't know if she's living there or what, unless her husband died. But she might take care of Ma. I don't know."

The fort was in sight, and the captain allowed his roan to pick up a canter. The party was soon dismounting near a high masonry wall that had withstood the fire the Mormons had set when they abandoned the fort in 1857. The black smudge of smoke was still evident on the stones, contrasting with the light wood of the new palisade. A private came to lead the captain's gray away, and Captain Smith, Byington's second in command, came to his side.

"The courier left for Fort Hall, sir, and a party of trappers came in this morning. Said they were caught in the storm yesterday, and one man drowned in the river east of here."

"Did they bring the body in?"

"No, sir, I sent four men out with them."

"Very good." Byington dismissed him and turned to the men behind him. "Jake Sherman, Mr. Zale, you may follow me. Pilcher, I suppose you'd better come, too as a witness for your contingent. There's not room for many more in my office."

He strode away without looking back. Jake threw Laura an apologetic glance and followed the captain. Corporal Markheim jumped to attention as they entered.

"Mail distributed, Corporal?" Byington asked, heading straight for safe.

"Yes, sir."

"At ease."

Markheim sat down and went back to his paperwork, but took curious glances at Jake and the two bearded Mormons.

"Here we go." Byington gave the dial a final spin and opened the safe door.

Jake leaned in close and looked past him. It took a moment for it to register in his brain that the safe was empty.

Chapter 32

"Markheim!" Byington roared.

The corporal stumbled to his feet. "Y-yes, sir?"

"What happened to the documents I left in this safe?"

"Lieutenant Smith removed them this morning, sir."

Byington clenched his teeth. "Get the lieutenant."

"Yes, sir." Markheim all but ran out the door.

Jake's heart sank. He watched the captain silently. There had to be some crazy mix-up. Smith couldn't be in on this preposterous plot.

The lieutenant arrived panting.

"You wanted me, sir?"

"Yes. Where are the documents I left in the safe?"

"I sent them to Fort Hall, sir. That's what you ordered."

Byington sat down slowly, and Smith stood nervously at attention, his eyes on the territorial map behind the captain's desk.

"What does this mean?" Pilcher asked.

Byington sighed. "There was a packet of dispatches to go to Fort Hall. The courier was delayed here because of the storm. He was about to set out this morning when I left—" He pulled out his pocket watch and looked at it. "That's three hours ago. Apparently he took the bill of sale with him by mistake." He glared at Smith.

Smith gulped. "There was a loose paper beneath the packet, sir. I—I thought it fell out of the bundle, and I stuck it in the—I'm sorry, sir."

Byington put his hand to his forehead for a moment, then stood up. "Dismissed, lieutenant. Jake, I'm sorry. This is partly my fault. I should have marked the paper plainly on the outside, or at least told the captain about it. It slipped my mind entirely this morning."

"It's all right, sir."

Zale stepped forward triumphantly. "No, it is *not* all right. You people have been putting me off since last evening, and I've had enough nonsense. There's no bill of sale here because there never was a bill of sale." He turned to Pilcher. "Isn't it obvious? These two men are related. I don't care what Byington's position is, he's obviously trying to protect his son-in-law from being charged as a horse thief and a kidnapper."

Pilcher looked warily from Zale to Byington. "I just don't know what to believe, Isaac."

Zale snorted. "You'd believe these gentiles over one of your own people?" He stormed outside, and Jake and the others followed. Laura came to him immediately.

"What is it? What's wrong?"

Jake drew in a deep breath. "Seems the bill of sale got dispatched to Fort Hall by accident."

"Fort Hall? That's insane."

"Tell it to Captain Smith."

"Smith? He's not that stupid."

Jake lifted his shoulders in resignation.

"Jake, you have to do something."

"I'm doing all I can, sweetheart."

"I'm sorry. Jake, I've been praying all morning."

"Then don't worry." He reached out with his good hand and tugged at her braid. "It's a setback, but things will work out in time." He reached up gingerly and fingered the knot on the back of his head.

"Are you in a lot of pain? Maybe you should see that medical fellow?"

"I'll be all right."

Zale had rounded on his own men angrily. "I say it's time we go home."

And good riddance, Jake thought.

"What about Red, Pa?" Rufus whined.

"Red goes with us. There's no proof he shouldn't." Zale strode toward where Coleman held the stallion.

Pilcher looked apologetically at the captain. "Well, sir, since you seem to have no evidence to the contrary..."

Byington glared at him. "Hold off. I'll send a detachment out after the courier. They should be able to catch up with him by tonight and be back tomorrow evening."

"No!" Zale plucked the reins from Coleman's hand and led the stallion toward Byington. "I've waited long enough. I'm not staying here another two days while you cook up another story. I'm riding out of here now on this horse, and that woman—" He pointed at Iris, and she shrank behind Laura. "--that woman is going with us, although I can't say I like her behavior on this expedition. I'm not sure I want to take her back into my house after her wanton display toward this scoundrel." His scathing glance at Edward seethed with contempt.

Jake saw Ed's stricken look and Rufus's new resolve.

"She's my bride to be," Rufus said, looking around at the others, as though not accustomed to speaking out firmly. "We ain't leaving here without her, mister."

The captain stiffened, and Jake reached out lightly to touch his sleeve. "A word, sir." They stepped aside with Laura, and Jake quietly made his appeal. "Captain, please don't let them take Miss Perkins. I know we don't want trouble, and the horse isn't that important. It's a business loss that I can swallow, though it would taste bitter."

Laura's hand sneaked into Jake's, and he clasped it firmly as he continued. "But you can't let them ride out of here with that young woman. It wouldn't be moral, sir, and she's trying her best to obey the Lord. If we turn her over to the Zales, no telling what they'll do to her once they're away from here, and she'll find it hard to trust the Lord to protect her any longer."

"I agree, son."

Jake nodded gratefully. The captain had always listened to him, from their first meeting, and he prayed he was on solid ground now. He didn't like implying that they should use force if needed, but he saw no other way to solve this crisis.

Byington turned to Pilcher. "Sir, if you don't want to wait while we secure the proof, I suggest you leave quietly. And if Mr. Zale insists on recovering the stallion, then he must pay Thomas Sherman back the money received."

"There was no money received!" Zale glared at Jake with murderous fury.

"I was there when the Shermans came to buy the horse," Iris said. Everyone turned to stare at her, and she shrank back, not toward Laura, but toward Edward. He stood firm beside her.

"So was I," he said. "And we didn't steal Iris. She left of her own accord."

"I even left a note, explaining that I was going away." She turned pleadingly to Captain Byington. "Please sir, I beg you, let me stay here."

"Isaac," Pilcher began uneasily.

Zale raised his hand. "Let's not be hasty here. On one side you've got me and my son as witnesses. On the other, Sherman and his brother."

"And his wife," Laura said with scathing contempt.

Zale could not meet Laura's cutting gaze, but he hurried on, "Maybe there's a way to settle this without hard feelings."

"You have a suggestion?" Pilcher asked.

"Yes, a simple one." Zale's eyes glittered. "A race."

Jake was instantly alert. What was the trickster up to now?

"A race?" Pilcher asked.

"That's right. My Red against Sherman's big gray."

Laura whirled around and whispered, "Spook can beat him, Jake!"

"Easy, now," Jake said. "I'm not a gambling man, Mr. Zale."

Zale shrugged. "Suit yourself." He pulled the reins up over Blaze's neck as if preparing to mount the stallion.

"Hold on!" Byington cried. A knot of soldiers had gathered during the debate, and he motioned to Coleman. "Get Captain Smith. I want a full guard on these men while we step inside and discuss this in private. And send for Murphy. I want Sherman's wrist looked at."

Hal hurried toward the soldiers, and Jake saw several of them move between Zale's party and the entrance to the fort.

"Mr. Pilcher," said Byington, "I'd like to discuss this proposition with the Shermans and Miss Perkins in my office. If you gentlemen would like to get in out of the cold, I'll make the mess hall available to you. There will be coffee in there."

Pilcher looked to Isaac Zale.

"Ten minutes," Zale said grudgingly. He made no sign that he saw the armed soldiers gathering, but Jake had no doubt he noticed.

As soon as they were in Byington's office, Ed buttonholed his brother eagerly. "It wouldn't be gambling, Jake. Spook can take that crowbait any day. Blaze is so fidgety, he wears himself out. He's fast, it's true, but if you made it a long distance, say out to our ranch and back, Spook would win hands down."

"Edward, think! You're not just talking about the horse and the money Laura and I would lose. You're talking about Iris. You do care about her, don't you?"

Ed colored and glanced toward Iris. Her eyes were downcast, but she seemed to be waiting to hear what he would say. "I expect I do."

"Then use your head. You could ruin everything by giving in to Zale on this foolish stunt."

Iris raised her chin and looked Jake in the eye. "But God has the power to make Spook win, doesn't He? Laura said God always does what's best, even if we don't understand it."

Jake looked helplessly at Laura. "Well, that's true, but—"

"God wouldn't let a liar defeat someone who was telling the truth, would he?"

Jake ran his hand through his hair. The bump on his head was throbbing now, sending pounding waves of pain through his skull. "The question is, Miss Perkins, can we have a fair contest with an unfair man?"

Hal came in and closed the door. Byington eyed him expectantly.

"Twenty men in place, sir. Murphy is on wood detail, but he should be here soon."

"Good. Sit down, Jake. You're not seriously thinking of taking Zale up on this, are you?"

"Of course not! If we lose, Iris goes back to who knows what horrors, and I lose a great deal of money on that foolish horse." He laid his hat on the captain's desk and brushed the hair back from his forehead. "I wish I'd never laid eyes on him."

"We won't lose," Laura insisted, her eyes dancing. "Spook and I can beat anyone, Jake. You know it's true."

Jake frowned at her. "Spook and you? I won't let you ride against one of them."

"But *you* can't do it, Jake. You're hurt. And Spook would do anything for me. I can do it easily. Zale will never come near us!"

"What do you say, Miss Perkins?" Captain Byington asked.

Iris's face wrinkled, and she shook her head. "I don't know. I'm confused. If God promises to protect those who believe in Him, why don't we just show those men up, like Laura says? But Mr. Sherman sounds as if he's not sure we would win. Wouldn't God want us to win?"

Ed looked cautiously at the captain. "Sir, maybe this would be a good time for prayer."

Byington nodded. "Of course. We can't go into something this important without God's guidance."

Iris's perplexed expression was banished. "Please, sir, let's do that. I don't know what's right, but God must."

"Yes, child. He knows everything." They all bowed their heads, and Captain Byington said quietly, "Lord, we've got some tangled circumstances here, and we don't want to be foolish. But we would

184

dearly love to see You show Your power today. Give us Your wisdom. Amen."

"Amen," they all echoed.

Iris's eyes shone. "Captain Byington, I'm willing to submit to their terms."

"Are you certain?"

"Yes. I know God will be with me now, no matter what. But I also believe Spook will win."

Jake lifted his head suddenly. "Hal, get out there and set a couple of troopers to watch the horses, will you? I don't want anyone from the other side going near Spook."

"Then you'll agree to the race?" Ed asked as Hal stepped outside.

Jake sighed. "I don't know. I can't afford a loss."

"We won't lose," Laura repeated. "Spook has pulled us through before, and God can use him to do it again."

"What if we lose the money, sweetheart?"

"As you said, it would be difficult, but it wouldn't kill us. And you and Ed and Hal can go catch that old mustang stallion in the hills for the ranch if need be, but it won't come to that."

"Besides, Laura says *what-if's* aren't allowed," Iris said.

Jake bit his upper lip. Iris's innocence seemed genuine, but it rankled him. Laura was a born optimist, and she had said those very words to him several times. Apparently her short acquaintance with Iris had been long enough to pass on her philosophy. His head felt like it was splitting, thanks to the sturdy fence post he had landed on when Blaze tossed him.

"I just can't think straight," he said. "Laura, I know if it was you they were threatening to haul off, I'd never take the chance. We can't risk it with Iris."

"But, God can do anything. Can't he?" Iris looked from him to Laura, a shadow of disillusionment hovering in her face once more.

Captain Byington cleared his throat. "I think Jacob is right, Miss Perkins. God *is* all-powerful, and He promises us His protection. But

He also gives us common sense and expects us to avoid taking foolish risks. You wouldn't drink a bottle of poison thinking God would protect you from its ill effects, would you?"

"I – I don't know."

Laura squeezed Iris's hand. "Father's right. I got all excited because I love a contest, and I think we could do it. But that would be trusting in Spook's strength, and in our own cleverness, not in God's power."

Jake nodded slowly. "That's what I meant. God is plenty powerful enough to make Spook win a race, no matter what, but He's also powerful enough to help the person who is doing right triumph without any machinations."

"What does that mean?"

Jake smiled at Iris, noticing how pleasant her earnest face was. Maybe Edward wasn't so hare-brained after all.

"I just mean, God could strike those six men out there dead anytime, if He wanted. He doesn't need for us to do all sorts of difficult, tricky things to make this turn out right."

Iris put her hand timidly on Jake's shoulder. "Mr. Sherman, I appreciate so much what your family has done for me. I set out to help you, but when I asked for your help in return, I caused you a lot of trouble."

"We don't blame you." Jake smiled at her. He was feeling very tired, and the pain seemed to be worse. He held his throbbing wrist, and the warmth seemed to help a little. He wished the captain would just take over and make all the decisions for him, but he knew it was up to him. He looked around at their expectant faces. "All right. No race. We're in the right here, and we don't have to do something like that to prove it. Ed, Laura, you were witnesses to the sale. Captain, you know I don't lie."

"Of course you don't," Byington agreed. "There was never a question, Jake. I didn't open that bill of sale and look at it, but I held it in my hand, and I know you and Laura are being truthful."

Jake nodded. "Fine. Then let's tell them there's no race, and we'll see what the Lord will do next."

There was a knock on the door, and Hal opened it.

"Three men are at the gate asking for Jake Sherman," said a cavalryman.

Jake and Byington looked at each other. Jake shrugged. The captain went to the door. "Civilians?"

"Yes, sir. Like the ones yonder."

Byington looked over his shoulder at Jake. "Do you feel like entertaining more Saints?"

Jake gritted his teeth. "I don't like it."

"I'll have them brought in here."

"Does Zale know they're here?" Jake asked.

Byington lowered his voice and spoke to the trooper again, then turned back to Jake. "Zale and the others are in the mess hall. My men are detaining the three at the gate. Shall we step out there? I'll go with you. There's not enough room in here, anyway."

Jake stood up slowly and began to button his coat, fumbling with one hand. Laura took over, fastening it quickly. He winked at her and put his hat on.

"Be careful, Jake."

He slipped his arm around her for an instant and squeezed her. "Can't get much worse, can it?"

Chapter 33

Laura came to Iris and grasped her hand. "I'm sorry, Iris. I never should have gotten excited about the idea of the race. It would have been idiotic to even give them a chance to get you back in their power. You're far too precious to risk losing."

"That's right," Ed said softly, and Iris felt her cheeks flush.

"Thank you," she whispered, sneaking a glance at him.

"Sometimes I get a little carried away," Laura admitted.

"Impetuous," Edward agreed. Laura arched her eyebrows at him, and he added hastily, "At least, I've heard you might have been that way when you were younger. Not now. A long time ago."

Laura laughed.

"You should sit down," Iris said, but Laura shook her head. "Nonsense."

"I don't think I can sit still until this is settled," Iris said woefully.

"Well, as far as my father is concerned, it's settled now," Laura assured her. "No one is dragging you out of this fort."

The door opened, and Hal Coleman leaned in, smiling. "Miss Perkins, a surprise for you."

"Me?" Iris stared at him, but he stepped back and another man pushed through the doorway. He was thin and stoop-shouldered, she could see, even in his thick woolen overcoat. His beard was ragged and graying, and his hat was drawn down over shaggy hair. But his eyes were the violet-brown eyes she loved.

"Pa!" Two steps and she was in his arms, sobbing uncontrollably. Someone tucked a handkerchief in her hand, and when she was able to push away and really look at him, they were alone in the small room.

Her breath came in short gasps. He looked ill, and much older than she remembered.

"I didn't know what became of you," he said gruffly, and Iris saw that tears had formed in his eyes as well.

"I thought you were dead, Pa. It's been so long! Where were you?"

Her father sighed. "Where haven't I been? We had a rough time of it, daughter. Didn't know as we'd make it for a while there."

"Pa! Is Conrad all right?"

"Sure. He's waiting outside. That there officer was afraid you'd faint if we both come in at once."

"What kept you so long?"

"Our guides turned on us and shot one of our fellows. Stole our mules and left us in the high country. But we got out. Conrad stuck with me, every step of the way. He half carried me, the last of it."

"How did you manage to survive?"

He shrugged. "Et a few lizards. We finally hobbled into one of the settlements down Ely way. They took us in and sent word to Salt Lake. Brigham sent a party down to bring us to him."

"When?" Iris asked.

"Three weeks ago, maybe."

"But I was at the Zales' then."

"So I was told later on. They told us at first to rest up, but I was anxious to see you. Conrad and I went by the old house, and they'd given it over to some come-lately family. I hollered to the bishop, I'll tell you. Finally they said to rest easy at Salt Lake, and they'd fetch you. Didn't say nothing about getting our furniture and things back, though."

"No one came for me, or if they did, I wasn't told."

"I thought you was with Elder Whipple," her father said, shaking his head. "After I'd been in Salt Lake a week, here comes Whipple, atellin' me he'd took you off to this other ranch where you was to meet your husband. That didn't make me happy."

"Oh, Pa, I'm so glad you're back!"

He held out his arms, and Iris crumpled into them again.

"They got you married off, have they?"

She gulped. "No, not yet, but they mean to. I'm in an awful fix, and my friends are, too. They've tried to help me, but having me here has made things worse for them." She pushed away suddenly. "How did you know I was here at Fort Bridger?"

"When the elders told me you were at Zale's ranch, I went there, but Mrs. Zale said you ran away, and then the other sister said you'd been kidnapped by some horse trader. I couldn't make out what had happened, but they said Zale took some men to come get you from a farm on this side of the pass. I stopped at the next place to get some help, and Philip Gluck said that couldn't be the way it was, that this Sherman who was buying horses was a good fella. He said Sherman lived close to Fort Bridger, and he came with me to find you."

Iris put her hand to his cheek. "Mr. and Mrs. Sherman have been wonderful to me. It's those Zales who've got me running, Pa. They want me to marry Rufus, their son, but he's mean and uncouth, and I can't abide him. He whips their horses, and I've seen him hit his little brother." She bit her lip, but her tears were unstoppable.

"Can't believe Elder Whipple approved this," her father said. "I left you with him thinking he was a man of sense. But I found out in Salt Lake they're pressuring all the elders now into plural marriages. Whipple apologized, but he told me ...." He eyed her keenly.

"What, Pa?"

"Said he figured I'd rather have you wed to a young fellow like Zale's son than a old codger like him."

She drew back, appalled. "Oh, no, Pa. There was never any question of that."

"You don't know everything, girl."

Iris tried to accept all he'd said. The grimness of it made her feel sad and weary.

191

"But Elder Whipple said Rufus was chosen for me."

"He wasn't the first choice. Whipple fought hard for you to go to a bachelor or a widower, Iris. He stood by you, and you can be thankful for that."

"He defied the church for me?"

"He's in danger of losing his position."

"For taking me to the Zales?"

"That and refusing to take a second wife. The prophet says the elders who want to remain in good standing have to do it."

She shuddered. "Please don't make me go back, Pa."

"You'll come with me now." He stroked her long, dark tresses. "I wouldn't choose that life for my girl. We'll find you some nice young man you can get along with. None of this sister wife in an old man's house business. If you're to be married, it's going be as the first wife of a likely young fellow with good prospects, make no mistake. I won't give you to a dimwitted brawler, either. If you don't like young Zale, that's it as far as I'm concerned. He's out of the running."

Iris shuddered. The idea of being any man's first wife was repugnant to her now, and she knew she would rather be solitary the rest of her life than go back. She was ready to defy the elders, and her father, too, if need be, and take the consequences. "Thank you, Pa, but—" she took a deep breath. "I want to stay here."

He froze for an instant, then leaned down to look closely at her eyes. "You want to leave Deseret? You can't, daughter."

"Why not?"

"Because—because it's part of God's plan."

Iris shook her head. "I'm just beginning to learn about God, Pa. I'm starting to have opinions of my own. Some things I've seen don't make sense with what I read in the Bible. I don't want to go back. Ever."

They stood for a long moment, appraising each other.

"Are you saying you've lost your faith?"

Iris looked away, then back at his unrelenting eyes. "No, Pa. I've found it."

Her father blinked. "I don't know as women are allowed to have their own opinions, Iris. Anyway, the Saints want you to go back. The captain said there's an elder here with Zale to fetch you."

"Well, I think they mostly came for the horse Jake Sherman bought, Pa. He paid for it, fair and square, but Brother Zale is claiming he stole it. It's not true. I know he paid for that horse. Then Brother Zale said he'd race the stallion against Mrs. Sherman's gray, and whoever won got the stallion, and me to boot. But Mr. Sherman wouldn't hear of it. He said he's not gambling with people's lives."

"The Saints would gamble away my daughter?" Perkins stared in puzzlement. "Are you certain that's what they meant?"

"Yes, Pa, and we almost fell for it. But then we prayed, and the captain and Mr. Sherman both said God wouldn't want us to do it that way, that He'll show us a better way to set things right."

"A race," said Perkins.

She nodded. "Mr. Sherman, that is, Jake Sherman, says it wouldn't be right, even though God could make it so we'd win, easy as pie."

"Did he now?"

"Yes. And I believe it. Pa, I don't like to speak against people, but I don't think you'd like the way I was treated at the Zales', or at the Whipples', though it wasn't too bad there."

Her father breathed in deeply. "I don't know what to make of all this, daughter. I don't know if these gentiles have filled your head with some rebellious craziness, or ..."

Suddenly Iris felt afraid again. "Or what, Pa?"

Her father didn't answer. His forehead was wrinkled as he stood looking speculatively toward the map on the wall behind the desk. "A race, you say."

Chapter 34

Ed accepted Philip Gluck's handshake with reluctance.

"Good to see you again," Gluck said.

Ed nodded, uncertain as to where Gluck's loyalties lay.

The young man shook his head and looked toward Jake. "I don't know why Zale's got this idea about the trade not being legal, but I figured I'd bring Brother Perkins along to try and find his daughter, and if I could, I'd see you two and find out what's what."

"That's what we'd all like to know," Jake laughed.

Ed nodded. "The last two days have been wild."

Philip said, "Well, I'm reserving judgment until I hear the whole story."

"Speaking of stories, I'll wager you've got a good one to tell," Ed said to Iris's brother. Conrad Perkins had stood quietly beside Philip, listening to them talk. His brown eyes had the same velvety, violet shade that his sister's had, and his hair was a shade lighter than hers. He was thin, and Ed thought he looked like he could use a good meal and a warm bunk.

Conrad swallowed and nodded. "Yes, sir. Reckon I do."

"Iris said you and your father left last spring to prospect for the Saints?"

"That's right. We scouted for minerals all summer, and saw a heap of country. We found some deposits of lead and iron. Kept thinking we'd find something better over the next ridge. We got clear over to the Monitor Range, and then we had a catastrophe."

"What happened?"

"Some Indians were guiding us. Said they knew a place where we'd find silver for sure, so we had 'em take us, but they went farther and farther into the wilderness. They stole our mules when we were deep in the mountains and left us afoot there. My father and I were a long time getting back to civilization. We nearly died of thirst at first, then we found water, but came close to starving. Our boots wore through before the cold weather set in. Then we'd like to have froze."

"Your pa looks worn out," Ed said.

"He is, but when we got back to Salt Lake and couldn't find Iris, he insisted we come after her." He looked toward the captain. "Have you seen her? Is she all right?"

"Yes, son," Byington said. "She's in good health. A quick-witted, personable girl, your sister."

"Thank you. Those women at the Zale place—well, they weren't making much sense, but we were afraid Iris had been manhandled and stolen away against her wishes. If you've been protecting her from the horse thieves, I thank you, sir."

"There are no horse thieves," the captain said gently. "Perhaps later on you'll get a chance to sit down with your sister and hear the whole story."

He looked up as the mess hall door opened and Pilcher, Zale and their companions came outside. Zale spotted Philip and came slowly toward them.

"Well, now. Brother Gluck, what brings you here?"

Philip shook hands with Zale. "Oscar Perkins showed up at my place yesterday, looking for his daughter. Said your lady told him she was over this way somewheres. I thought I'd ride along with him and his boy." He nodded toward Conrad.

Rufus pushed forward beside his father. "Iris's father's here?"

Isaac quelled him with a riveting scowl.

"That's good news," Pilcher said jovially, but his smile faded as he looked at Zale. "Don't you think so, Isaac? He'll bring her back, and she'll stop wanting to leave the church."

"I don't rightly know," Zale admitted. "I'm thinking that girl's got a mind of her own."

"That's right," Ed said coldly. "She had enough spunk to leave your place."

"Edward." Jake was quiet, but firm, and Ed nodded slightly, acquiescing to his brother's authority. "Here they come now. We'll see what they have to say."

Iris came from headquarters with the stooped, graying man. When she saw her brother, she gasped and ran to him.

"Conrad!"

The young man embraced her with a sob. "You all right, Iris?"

"Yes! Are you?"

Captain Byington stepped forward. "Well, Miss Perkins, this has turned out to be a happy day for you."

"Yes, sir." She looked toward her father and smiled tremulously.

Ed thought the smile was a little weak for a young woman reunited with the parent she had so desperately wanted to see. He edged around Jake to a spot that was a little closer to her. She glanced his way, and he tried to semaphore his sympathy with his eyes.

"What's all this about a horse race?" Perkins asked.

Iris caught her breath. Ed eyed Oscar Perkins, surprised he had caught wind of the proposal and trying to gauge his interest.

"Oh, it's nothing," Byington said.

Iris flushed and appealed to the captain. "I mentioned it in passing, and father was taken with the idea. I'm sorry, sir. I wasn't promoting the race."

Byington frowned and said carefully, "Mr. Zale suggested a race as a means to settle a property dispute between him and Mr. Sherman, here, but Sherman's decided it's not in his best interest."

Zale turned angrily on Jake. "Oh, he has, has he? That's because he's a thieving fox."

Jake's jaw clenched, and Hal Coleman stepped between them. "Take it easy, Zale."

"It's time to end this foolishness," Byington said. "Jacob Sherman bought the stallion. The horse stays here. You gentlemen may leave, the sooner the better, and it's up to Miss Perkins and her father whether she stays or goes."

Perkins smiled. "Well, you got that part right, mister. I may have been away for a while, but I'm still her daddy, and I have the say on where my little girl goes and where she doesn't."

Ed could see that Laura was itching to light into Perkins, but Jake anchored her with his right hand, holding her arm.

"My wife and I have invited your daughter to stay with us for a while if she wishes, sir," Jake said. "Iris and Mrs. Sherman get along, and we thought she'd like to visit. For a change of scenery, you might say."

Ed's anxiety climbed as Perkins looked Jake over from head to toe, his eyes glittering. Laura was obviously restraining her wrath, but said nothing, and Ed decided she was right. Let Jake handle it. But Iris had been sure her father would rescue her from her untenable situation if he were able. Had she been completely wrong?

"Well, now," Perkins said slowly, "It seems to me someone's been filling my daughter's head with strange notions about the Bible and pernicious doctrines. Would that be you and your hospitable wife?"

Jake's chin came up half an inch. "I assure you, sir, the only things Iris has learned in our house are truths straight from God's word."

Perkins's eyes narrowed, and they all waited. He turned suddenly to where two troopers stood watching the cluster of saddled horses.

"That the stallion?"

"Yessirree, that's my Red," Zale said heartily.

"I tell you what," Perkins said to Jake, "I don't know the what or the why of this disagreement, but I hear my daughter saying you won't race even though God would make you win if you did."

Jake blinked. "Well, that's not exactly—"

Perkins cut him off with a wave of his hand. "I've had some strange experiences myself this past year, and I came from Ely and Galena thinking I'd fetch my girl and leave the territory."

A light leaped into Iris's violet eyes. "Pa! You didn't tell me."

"What's stopping you?" Jake asked quietly.

"I just don't know what's right and what's not anymore. I don't know what's true and what's false. But here's my Iris telling me God can make the right side win. Well, sir, I say, let's have the race. No one will get hurt, and God can answer my question."

"What question is that?" Pilcher asked uneasily.

"If I should keep on with the Saints or leave."

Conrad stepped to his father's side, a troubled expression on his face. "Pa, don't talk like that. This here's an elder."

"Hush. I'm telling you all this: if that red horse wins, I don't rightly care who keeps him, but I'll take my daughter and go back into Deseret and do whatever the elders tell me." He nodded, closing his eyes for an instant. "Even if they send me back to the mines."

"What about Iris, Pa?" Conrad asked, his voice cracking with anxiety.

Ed looked at Iris, but she was staring down at the dirt, her expression one of intense pain.

"If they win, we'll trust the elders to find the right man for her."

That would be my son," Zale said.

Oscar Perkins stood looking at him for a moment. Both men's eyes smoldered with dislike, and Ed thought Perkins would protest, but at last he said, "Fine. If he's the man the elders pick for her, I'll accept that."

Iris's shoulders shook, and Ed longed to comfort her, but he was afraid if he acted in a proprietary manner the Saints would spring on him again. With relief he saw Laura leave Jake's side. She eased up quietly beside Iris and slipped her arm around her.

"And if Sherman wins? What do you say then?" Zale was testy to the point of anger, but for once he held himself in control.

"If Sherman wins, then I'll let Iris call the shots. If she wants to stay here, so be it. But not unless her God comes down on her side."

"Pa," Conrad said anxiously, touching his father's shoulder, but Oscar shook off his hand.

199

Jake stared at the older man grimly. "Give me some time to discuss this with my family."

"No!" Zale leaped to Perkins's support. "We've waited and we've wrangled and we've chewed the fat. It's time to act."

Jake looked at Laura, then at Ed. Ed held his breath.

"All right," Jake said. "We'll race."

Chapter 35

Rufus jumped into the air whooping with glee. At the noise, Blaze lunged to the end of his rope and neighed, kicking the horse next to him. The reaction went down the line of waiting horses as they jostled each other, nipped, kicked, and squealed.

Riley and the other trooper assigned to watch the horses walked up and down the line, speaking firmly to the animals until they settled down.

"We'll need to set the terms," Jake said.

Zale grinned. "Brother Pilcher, you see to it."

"Captain Byington?" Pilcher asked tentatively.

Byington nodded and stepped forward. "Shall we go into my office, Mr. Pilcher?"

Jake drew Laura and Hal with him a few steps away. Ed hung back and looked at Iris. She was standing near her brother and father, but she was watching him. Ed started toward her, and she took a hesitant step forward. He took that as an indication that she was willing to come with him. He reached for her hand and led her to where his brother waited. Oscar and Conrad stood forlorn between the two groups, but Iris seemed to have momentarily forgotten them, and Ed turned his back on them. Time to befriend them later, when and if Iris showed him that she wanted him to be friends with her family.

Now she was concentrating on Jake, looking to him anxiously as she rejoined their group.

"But, Mr. Sherman, I thought you were against the race."

"I was, Iris. I still am. But things have changed." Jake hesitated. "I don't think it's right, but your Pa has us over a barrel. If we don't race, he'll take you back to Utah, and he may be angry enough to be mean."

"He might even hand you back over to the elders and Zale," Laura said tightly, and Iris shivered.

"I don't know," she admitted. "He's changed. I just don't know."

Ed squeezed her hand. He remembered how blithely he had told her he would speak to her father, given the opportunity. But Jake was right. Everything had changed. Oscar Perkins was no longer the missing protector. He might be his daughter's worst enemy. Part of Ed wanted to attack him, and the other part wanted to whisk Iris away from the turmoil, where she could live in peace and grow in her new faith, where he could love her and protect her. He knew that he had to come carefully to some better course of action than opposing her father.

"Do you want to go back with your Pa?" Jake asked. He was sympathetic, Ed could tell, but was giving Iris a chance to voice her wishes clearly. If she wavered in her desire to leave Utah, What would he do? The thought of losing her now was heartbreaking.

Slowly Iris shook her head. "No. I'm afraid to. Pa is so different from what he was last time I saw him." She looked up at Ed, and his heart jumped at the plea he saw. "I don't want to go back."

"What about your brother?" Jake asked. "Where does he stand in this?"

"I don't know. I haven't had a chance to talk to him."

Jake nodded. "I suspect he'll back your pa."

"We won't let them take you away." Ed determined to keep this promise if he died in the attempt.

"So, let's tell them I'll ride," Laura said with a smile.

Jake chuckled. "You? No, darlin'."

"Why not?" Laura's eyes danced as she eagerly made her case. "Spook's been standing there resting for an hour. The two of us are ready to go! We're an unbeatable team."

Jake laughed. "I don't think so."

Laura grabbed the front of his jacket. "Oh, Jake, you know I've raced against every horse in the remuda and beaten them, and that was before Father gave me Spook."

"This could get rough, Miz Sherman," Hal said softly. "I don't think a woman should go up against one of their men."

"Why not? It would serve them right to let a woman humiliate them."

Jake smiled. "Your pride is showing, sweetheart."

"Besides, these fellows are apt to play dirty," Ed agreed.

Iris shook her head emphatically. "Laura, you can't do this. What about the baby?"

There was silence as all eyes turned to Iris.

"Baby?" Jake asked, as though he'd been dropped into the middle of a different conversation. He looked blankly at Iris.

She put her hand to her mouth and looked beseechingly at Laura. "I'm sorry. I didn't mean—" She stared at Jake. "Oh, I'm so sorry."

"Baby?" Jake said again, staring at his wife until she met his gaze.

Laura stepped closer to him and slipped her hand through the crook of his arm. Her face colored, and she gave a nervous glance around at Ed and Hal, then in the direction of her father's office, but the door was shut firmly on his discussion with Pilcher.

She looked up at her husband and drew a deep breath. "I'm sorry, sweetheart. I wasn't trying to keep it from you, but I haven't had a minute alone with you since—well, since that night at the Glucks' ranch."

Jake nodded patiently. "So, this baby …?"

"Yes. I hope you're pleased."

Jake grinned. "You clever woman. I always knew you could do anything."

"But we are going through with the race, right?" Ed asked. He saw the flame of love simmering between Jake and Laura, and he knew this ought to be a moment when the family celebrated a miracle, but his heart was still anxious about Iris's fate.

"You are," Jake said, and Ed knew it was the right decision. It was his right to win Iris's freedom.

Laura bridled at the decision. "Jake, please, I can do this. I'm strong and healthy. I rode all over Utah with you last week, without any problems. I want to do it for Iris."

Jake raised his right hand and placed his index finger on her full lips, stilling her. "Mrs. Sherman, you are a beautiful, talented lady, and I love you. I know you're an infamous daredevil, and an extraordinary rider. But there'll be no breakneck rides for you today."

Laura's disappointment was palpable, and Ed thought it would sway Jake, but he had underestimated his brother. Jake silently raised his eyebrows, looking steadily down into Jake sat down on the step to the mess hall and closed his eyes for a moment. The stallion had thrown him hard to the ground in the dustup back at the ranch. He wouldn't have thought he could feel so nauseous and weak an hour after bumping his head. He took a deep breath, willing himself to make it through this endless, nonsensical day.

Laura's blue eyes.

"All right," she whispered.

Jake laughed. "Good girl." He bent to kiss her forehead. "Now, if you don't mind, I'm going to sit on that step over there. My head aches, and I'm feeling a mite wobbly."

~~~~~

"Jake, the medical man is here," Laura said.

He opened his eyes. Laura bent over him anxiously, and a trooper was strolling toward him, carrying a dilapidated leather bag.

"This the patient? Step inside and let me take a look, sir."

Captain Byington was just coming from his office with Elder Pilcher. "Jake, Laura, you join us when you're ready," the captain called.

Jake rose stiffly and went into the mess hall with Laura and Murphy, and sat down on the nearest bench. "You got anything in there for a headache?" he asked as he appraised the soldier.

Murphy winked, opened the bag, and pulled out a bottle of brandy.

Jake tried to shake his head, but it hurt too much.

"Put that away," Laura said. "My husband is not a drinking man."

"It's good medicine," Murphy insisted.

"My head's muddled enough." Jake squinted at him. "How about willow bark?"

The man laughed. "Afraid not. I can give you something to make you sleep for awhile."

Jake sighed. "Forget it." He reached for his hat.

"Wait, don't you want me to look at your arm?"

Jake smiled tightly. "That's all right. I already got an herb woman to put some leaves on it."

Laura jabbed him in the ribs, then laughed. "You will be all right, won't you?"

"Guarantee it. I just need a little recovery time."

He ambled out onto the parade ground, and Laura kept pace with him. He was sure she was worried about him, but she maintained a cheerful demeanor, and he concentrated on walking naturally.

"Well, Jake, did Murphy help you out?" Byington asked.

"Oh, yeah, I'm fine." He looked for something to lean on, but there was nothing close by, so he stood with his arm on Laura's shoulders, trying not to list too badly.

"You should have let me ride Spook," Hal said, coming up on his other side. "I could do it, you know."

Jake nodded judiciously, ignoring the searing pain in his skull. "Probably could, Hal, but if you'll pardon my saying it, you've got twenty or thirty pounds on Edward, and besides—" He looked to where Iris was standing, watching Ed cinch his saddle on Spook. "I think Miss Perkins has chosen her champion."

Chapter 36

Iris came and stood quietly watching Ed while he switched his saddle from Shakespeare to Spook. Pilcher and the captain had agreed on the race route: five miles to the Sherman ranch. The finish line would be in Jake's barnyard. No riding back to the fort.

He was acutely aware of Iris's presence, but unsure of what to say to her. Laura had come to tell her they would ride back to the ranch with Jake and her father to wait at the finish, then she left them together in awkward silence. Ed tightened the cinch on his light, cavalry-issue saddle, throwing a guarded glance at Iris. He wished things could be settled between them, like they were for the race, cut and dried. But this tangle over the horse had somehow superseded the human relationships at stake, and he didn't know what to say.

In the end, her father called to her. He and Conrad were riding out to the ranch with the other spectators. Iris threw a worried glance toward the group that was mounting for the ride, then turned back toward Ed. He seized her hands, conscious of the troopers watching him. He was sure to take some teasing later, no matter how the race turned out.

"Iris, just tell me. How do you feel about all this? About me?"

She blinked back tears and swallowed. "I want you to win. I want … a lot of things, Edward, but …"

"But what?"

"Most of all, I want the chance to know you better. If you lose, we won't have that."

"And if I win? Will you see me? Let me call on you, I mean? I want to have time to get to know you, too. Everything's happening too fast. I care about you, but it's too soon—"

"Yes. It's too soon, but the way things are going, everything seems urgent."

Ed nodded. "That's it exactly. I *have* to win." He couldn't force himself to think what would happen if he didn't.

Iris sobbed, and he knew she, too, was thinking the unthinkable.

"If Pa makes me go back, I won't forget you."

She turned and went quickly to where Laura was holding Tramp's reins for her.

As he waited, Ed couldn't keep the image of her violet eyes, misty with tears, from his mind. If he lost, would he have even a moment to say good-bye, or had he already said it? Laura grinned at him, confident he and Spook would win, but Iris's face drooped as they turned toward the ranch.

After the spectators left, Ed stood impatiently, rubbing Spook's muzzle and stroking his sleek gray neck, sliding his fingers under the coarse black mane where it fell on the near side. Spook snorted and rubbed his ear against Ed's wool uniform coat.

"Easy, there, you'll be taking my buttons off."

He had never found it easy to wait. Philip Gluck and Hal Coleman had stayed to supervise the two riders until the others had time to reach Jake's yard and fire the starting gun. At the ranch, Jake would mark a line of ashes in the snow. First horse over that line would be declared the winner. The wait seemed interminable. Ed didn't have a watch, but he figured they had at least another fifteen minutes to be sure the others had gotten there and the finish line was in place.

Ed didn't like the rules they had set. He and Jake had held out for a ten-mile race, to the ranch and back to Fort Bridger, to give Spook a solid edge. He was an endurance runner, while the sorrel was a high strung sprinter. But the Mormons had refused to give in to that condition, perceiving an unfair advantage. Instead, they would race from the fort's gate to Jake's corral. The captain had given in. At least the Utah men would be partway home after the race, without coming back to Fort Bridger. Ed suspected getting them away from the outpost was important to Captain Byington.

He went over the course in his mind. There were no shortcuts. The trail to the family homestead followed the river part of the way, and there was one place where they would have to ford the Black Fork, but it didn't concern him. Spook crossed it frequently, with no problems. Then they would skirt the foothills where he and Jake had spent countless hours as boys, trying to hatch a plot to catch the mustangs that grazed in the high meadows. Farther on, they would cross a smaller stream that tumbled down out of the mountains. It had been swollen with melting snow that morning, about half a yard deep and rushing along swiftly, but Laura had jumped Spook over it, and Ed was inclined to think Spook could do it again easily, even after running several miles. From there, they would dash through a rolling section of stunted pines, and out into the open again for a nearly flat stretch the last half mile to the ranch. They would leave the well-worn trail that continued westward and turn in at a wagon track Ed and Jake's father had started thirteen years ago. The ranch house and barn were tucked into a serene little pocket at the end of the valley, just above the Black Fork's high water line.

Laura had given him a few hasty words of advice before riding out with Jake and the others to witness the end of the race. *He hates to follow another horse*, she'd told him. *Get him out in front and let him go. He'll do the rest.* She didn't seem to begrudge him the honor of riding, now that Jake had made the decision. She'd advised Ed to give Spook a chance to drink before the others left for the ranch, but nothing after that, and she kissed him on the cheek. *We'll take care of Iris for you. Just think about winning*, she'd whispered.

And young Rufus Zale was riding against him. Ed was glad in a way, although Rufus's heavier father might have been easier to defeat. He suspected that was why the young man had been chosen. Still, he didn't think Rufus was the horseman he was. Ed lived in the saddle, while Rufus dug canals and sheared sheep. He remember the way the young man had ogled Iris, and he was glad he would have a legitimate forum in which to deal Rufus a sound defeat.

He fingered the braided reins. It was Laura's bridle, and the soft, reddish leather matched her ornate saddle. He'd slung that on Shakespeare for his sister-in-law.

Laura was definitely a good influence on Jake, he decided. Before she came into his life, Jake had had a reputation of being a tough, silent loner who knew Indians better than any other white man in the territory. Men who knew him liked him, but not many men knew him. He seemed more outgoing now, and Ed's own admiration for his brother had grown. Jake had always like to read, but he'd kept his thoughts to himself. Now he showed a softer side that Ed had never suspected. To look at him, you wouldn't peg him as a family man, but that's what he was becoming. A baby on the way. Ed smiled. They would have to write to Vivian and Jane with the news.

Again he felt a longing for a home and a family of his own. If Jake could do it, why couldn't he? The idea of marriage would have scared the daylights out of Ed a year ago. Now it was looking pretty good.

He couldn't help thinking of Iris. So much had happened that day. A few short hours ago, he'd held her in his arms, and she'd seemed to favor a courtship. Now that her father was on the scene, she seemed frightened again. Ed wished he could see her when she wasn't terrified. That might take time. Making her feel secure and safe would be an arduous job, but he wanted to take it on. More than anything, he wanted to win Iris, and to do that, he had to win the race.

Coleman strolled toward him, looking at his pocket watch. "Two minutes."

Ed took a deep breath and checked the saddle girth once more. "I'm counting on you, fella."

Spook nickered and nuzzled his shoulder. Ed led him toward the gate, and Rufus came across the parade ground, leading Blaze. The stallion pulled at the reins, and Rufus slapped his cheekbone.

"Hold on, you beast!"

Good, thought Ed. *He's scared of the horse.*

Every trooper not on duty had turned out to witness the race, and a dozen of them were clustered at the starting line to cheer Ed on. He grinned at their good-natured gibes as he mounted. A few trappers had joined the crowd, and a handful of Indians who had their lodges set up outside the fort's wall. Ed suspected there was a great deal of betting going on.

By the rules, neither rider was allowed to carry weapons, and Ed had already stripped his equipment to the minimum to give Spook every possible advantage. Now he peeled off his heavy coat and tossed it to Corporal Markheim, who was watching eagerly with the other cavalrymen. Ed shivered, but he knew he could stand the cold for the duration of the race, and the wool coat must weigh six or eight pounds. He kept his battered hat and leather gloves.

"Y'all keep that hoss on the track, now," called Riley, the Texan wrangler who worked with Coleman.

"Don't fall off, Sherman," Corporal Markheim said. "That's an order."

The men laughed, and Ed joined in half-heartedly. If only this was one of their impromptu races that didn't really matter.

Spook stood patiently, and just for an instant, Ed wondered if the big gelding really had the fire and stamina Laura claimed he had. But she and Jake, and even Hal, had regaled him with stories of Spook's valor and speed, and he decided to lighten the load of his thoughts by discarding the doubts.

I'm not putting my trust in the horse, Lord, he prayed silently. *You're the one who has to show Iris and her father what You can do.*

Blaze sidestepped as Rufus mounted, jostling Spook's hindquarters. The gray retaliated by wheeling and snapping at his haunches.

"Keep that devil away from me!" Rufus struggled to right himself in the saddle, and Ed laughed.

Blaze was gorgeous, there was no doubt about that. He tossed his head proudly. His legs were rounded with muscle, his chest deep and powerful. But he was already dripping sweat, and a lather was forming where the leather cinch connected the girth to the saddle.

Ed wondered how upset Jake would be if he lost the stallion. That was part of the bargain now. His brother and Zale had signed the agreement Captain Byington had dictated to Corporal Markheim. Whoever's horse crossed the finish line first was the owner of the sorrel stallion, with no more controversy.

And if he won, would his brother be able to apply a layer of manners to the fiery stallion? Jake could train any colt to behave, Ed had no doubt, but he wasn't sure this stallion was teachable. It was difficult to get a mature horse to break bad habits. Still, if anyone could do it, Jake could, and he knew his brother wouldn't put up with a mean horse for long.

Perhaps he would never have the opportunity. Ed would blame himself if he lost the race. The others would console him and assure him it was God's will, but he would never forgive himself if the beautiful, willful stallion and the frightened girl went back to Utah. He could save up his pay and reimburse Jake for the horse, even help him catch the wild paint stallion, but he knew he would never have another chance with Iris. He had to justify her hopes today, or his dream of a home with her, warm and loving like Jake and Laura's, would be lost.

~~~~~

"Ten seconds," Coleman called, and Gluck raised his rifle, pointing it skyward and toward the prairie. Ed shortened the reins a little and leaned forward in the saddle, centering his weight squarely over Spook's shoulders. He could feel Spook tense with anticipation. Blaze whinnied and pawed, and with great effort Rufus held him in check.

"Three, two, one—"

212

Gluck pulled the trigger. As Spook leaped forward, Blaze squealed and kicked him soundly in the ribs, barely missing Ed's leg. Spook grunted and kicked back. For an instant, Ed thought the race would be over, and both riders would land in a heap while the two horses faced off. But with a cry of pain, Blaze shot toward the trail. Ed straightened Spook and urged him forward.

The gray eagerly pursued Blaze. Ed squeezed him forward, angry that Rufus had taken the lead. But Rufus seemed to be off balance in the saddle, in danger of taking a tumble. Within seconds, Spook was on Blaze's heels.

Ed felt like he was flying. He'd never ridden so fast, and the wind tore his breath away. As Spook settled into a gallop that inched him up inexorably alongside the sorrel, Ed sensed that his mount could go faster yet, and he laughed.

Clinging to the saddle horn, Rufus looked over at him darkly. "Go, Red!"

The stallion pulled out another notch of speed, staying even with Spook, then slowly gaining. When his haunches came even with Spook's withers, he kicked again, and this time Spook swerved, avoiding the blow, but allowing Red to take a lead of several yards. Ed decided to save the gray's strength until there was plenty of space to pass without coming close to the stallion's menacing hooves and teeth.

There's time, he told himself. *Spook will come on strong when the stallion is flagging. That's when we'll make our move.*

He concentrated on the trail, reveling in Spook's powerful stride. The gray was hardly straining, his long legs pumping regularly, almost effortlessly, his ears pricked toward the laboring stallion before him. Ed could feel him press forward, ready to lengthen the stride.

"You love this, don't you, boy?" He laughed, slapping Spook's neck.

He knew that as soon as they were out of sight of the fort, Coleman and Gluck, with any troopers who could find an excuse, would follow, eager for news of the finish. He maintained the short gap between himself and Rufus for the first mile, holding Spook back a little when he came up too close to the sorrel's haunches.

The ford was in sight now, with the sunlight gleaming silver on the water. Blaze faltered for an instant at the brink, then splashed on across. The winding river was shallow and broad here, and sluggish most of the year. Ed had crossed it thousands of times, and gave Spook an encouraging squeeze. Spook never hesitated, but bounded in, loping against the drag of the water. The far bank was about two feet high, and they came up to Blaze as he scrambled up it. Spook snapped at the stallion as he rocketed past him, and Blaze squealed in protest.

Ed laughed and urged Spook on, loosening the reins. The gray pounded along the rutted trail. Wagons didn't come this way so much anymore, not nearly so many as there had been a few years ago, but the traffic was still enough to keep the trail torn up in the bottoms. The snow was nearly gone now, and Ed was no longer cold. The beating sun and the rush of his excitement had warmed him thoroughly. He leaned low and pictured the triumphant finish of the race, when he and Spook would streak into the barnyard at the ranch, and Iris would be waiting, her face flushed with pleasure and her smile only for him.

They tore into the wooded stretch, lengthening their lead. When Spook halted suddenly, nearly sitting back on his haunches, Ed lost his balance and almost fell out of the saddle. His heart thudded as he regained control. Spook stood uneasily, snorting and stepping lightly back and forth, facing a bend in the path. They were near the rolling hills now, and Ed remembered coming through here one night with his father and almost colliding with a bull elk. He patted Spook's withers.

"Easy, boy."

Spook whickered and stepped forward, his ears twitching with agitation. Ed heard Blaze's hooves pounding on the trail behind him. If they didn't move, the stallion would run over them.

Then Spook's whinny was answered from ahead. Ed let Spook go forward. Jake and some of the others must have waited to see who was leading, but it was a bad place for it. They should have stationed themselves out in the open.

As he rounded the bend, Ed glimpsed movement off the trail to his left, and stared. Several riderless horses were running up the slope, through the brush that dotted the broken hillside. It had to be the mustang band. Spook whinnied shrilly, and again was answered, but the horses were moving away, into the hills.

Suddenly Blaze was upon them, and Ed dug his heels into Spook's sides. The gray turned back to the task at hand, lowering his head and leaping forward, as if determined not to let the sorrel pass him again. The trail was narrow here, but Ed knew Rufus was only yards behind him. He could hear Blaze's labored breath and thudding hoofbeats.

They came around the edge of the hill and headed down toward the stream they called Three-Mile because it was that far from the fort. Blaze vied for the lead, working slowly up beside Spook again, but his sides were heaving, and he didn't try to kick this time.

They reached the bank of Three-Mile together, and Ed rose over Spook's withers in preparation for the leap. Just as the huge gray launched himself, Blaze jumped, too. Rufus was out of control, and the stallion took off at an angle, bumping hard against Spook's left side in midair, and sending a shock of pain through Ed's knee.

With a surprised grunt, Spook landed just short of the far bank and floundered, stumbling on the stony bottom of the stream. Blaze landed even harder, rolling onto his side before righting himself with no rider. Ed was barely able to comprehend what had happened before he knew he'd lost his stirrups, and as Spook gave a mighty heave up the bank, he nearly slid off backward. He managed to cling to the saddle as Spook lurched upward and then stood on the bank, shaking off the water.

"Whoa, Spook!" Ed reached down to guide his feet back into the stirrups. A pain shot through his knee again as he turned his foot.

"Help!"

Ed whipped his head around. He had forgotten about Rufus for an instant. The young man was several yards downstream, beating the surface with his arms.

"Stand up, you fool!" Ed rode Spook along the bank until he was even with Rufus. "Come on, stand up."

"I can't!" Rufus gasped and sprawled headlong again in the water, and Ed realized he was slipping on the stones in the stream bed.

"Come on, Spook."

Blaze was still thrashing about in the water above, and Ed signaled Spook to step down into the cold stream again. The big gray hesitated, but then obeyed, hopping and floundering as his hooves sought for purchase on the jumbled stones. Ed eased him toward Rufus.

"Take my hand. I'll pull you up."

Rufus lunged at him, but slipped again. Ed bent over as far as he could, but couldn't reach him. He had to keep Spook moving along with the current to stay even with Rufus.

He hesitated. Dismounting in the frigid stream was the last thing he wanted to do, but Rufus repeatedly lost his footing and slipped farther downstream. Ed knew there were deep pools along here, and if Rufus didn't get out of the water soon he might slide into one and drown. Spook stepped forward, but stumbled again, and Ed feared he was in danger of breaking a leg on the stones.

"Help me!" Rufus ducked beneath the water and resurfaced, spluttering.

Ed gritted his teeth and swung his right leg over the cantle of the saddle. When he stood on the streambed, the ice-cold water was over the tops of his tall boots by several inches, and pain stabbed through his knee as he put weight on it. He dropped the reins and slapped Spook's flank. "Get out of here, Spook."

Ed took a step, and his feet went out from under him. Floating with the current, he gathered his legs and jabbed them down, lifting his upper body free of the water again. The rocks were rounded and smooth, and the leather soles of his boots found no traction. He planted his feet as firmly as he could with each step and walked awkwardly toward Rufus, who had fetched up on a boulder and clung to it desperately.

Already Ed was losing the feeling in his toes. He grabbed Rufus's collar and jerked him upright.

"Come on!"

Rufus was shivering uncontrollably. "I can't feel my feet!"

Ed hauled him toward the shore.

Several yards upstream, Spook had climbed out again and paced back and forth along the bank, watching Ed. Blaze labored up the bank and stood shivering. When Spook high-stepped close to him, the stallion confronted him with an outraged neigh that was more of a scream. Spook reared and struck at the stallion with his front hooves. Ed stood immobile, afraid that the gray would catch a hoof in his reins.

"Red!" the boy gasped. "Get Red! If he gets away, Pa will kill me."

Ed stared at him in disgust. "Get him yourself." He pushed Rufus unceremoniously to the bank of the stream and heaved him up onto the dead grass. His knee wrenched painfully, and he decided he couldn't climb up the steep bank there, so he sloshed his way back to the spot where Spook had climbed out.

Blaze and Spook had edged away from them, kicking and lunging at each other. Ed felt an instant's panic. Spook was spirited, but compared to the stallion, he'd have said the gray was docile. Now he was fighting as violently as Blaze. Wincing, he sidled up the bank, holding on to a small willow and trying to avoid putting his full weight on his left leg.

"Spook!"

The horses were intent on their grudge match. From the corner of his eye, Ed saw Rufus gain the high ground and stand shivering and watching the fighting pair.

Ed put two fingers to his mouth and whistled sharply. Spook turned toward him, and Blaze took the advantage to bite Spook's flank. Spook shrieked and turned back toward his enemy.

"I've got to get Red," Rufus panted as he reached Ed's side, his teeth chattering.

"Oh, what are you worried about? If Spook doesn't kill him, he'll just mosey on back to your daddy's place." Ed felt a twinge of conscience, but the combination of the cold, fear for Spook's safety, the pain in his knee, and the possibility that he would lose the race made him reckless. The day he had thought so mild had become a mortal danger. His body was cooling fast, now that he'd been drenched in the icy stream.

They watched in fascination as the two horses faced off again and again, approaching and striking, then backing off. Ed didn't dare distract Spook again, for fear he would drop his guard and be seriously injured by the stallion.

From above them on the brush-covered hillside came a piercing whinny, and the combatants paused momentarily. Ed and Rufus turned to stare upward.

A spotted black and white horse stood regal on the hillside, his head high. He called again, his neigh echoing across the valley, and Ed caught his breath.

It was the master of the mustang herd, with his dark face, a white strip on his nose, and a tossing black and white mane and tail.

The paint horse galloped belligerently down the slope. Spook shifted uneasily, and Blaze's eyes flared as he laid his ears back and snorted disdain for the newcomer.

The wild stallion's Roman nose was just short of ugly. He wasn't sleek and rounded like the horses he approached, but he radiated authority. When he was within ten yards of them, Blaze let out a shrill, challenging whinny. Spook snorted and paced away, tossing his head. The only trouble was, he headed away from Ed, down the trail.

Chapter 37

"There goes your horse," Rufus said.

Ed's heart sank. Spook hadn't been afraid to face Blaze, but he obviously felt he'd met his match in the paint mustang. Spook picked up speed, and his flying black tail disappeared into the scrub pines. All Ed could do was watch helplessly as Blaze and the newcomer squared off, sizing each other up as they pawed and snorted.

Behind him, Ed heard hoofbeats. Hal and half a dozen other riders were approaching the stream at a gallop. Ed held up his hand, and as soon as Hal saw him, he reined in. Philip Gluck and the troopers slowed, too. Their horses sloshed across the ford and clambered up the bank.

"What happened?" Hal called, trotting Lady toward them.

Edward nodded toward where Blaze and the mustang were still eyeing one another perniciously.

"Wa-all now!" said Riley.

"Where's Spook?" Hal asked.

"Probably near home by now." Ed shook his head.

"Here." Hal tossed him his wool coat.

Ed shrugged into it. "Thanks. I'm freezing."

Hal turned to the others. "Somebody give Zale something to wear."

Gluck immediately stripped off his own coat and handed it to Rufus.

"So, what do y'all wanna do now?" Riley asked, lifting his hat to scratch his head.

One of the troopers pulled out his rifle. "Want me to drop that paint?"

"No!" Ed hollered.

"Not unless we have to," Hal agreed.

At that moment, the paint closed on Blaze with a snort, and they heard his teeth snap as the sorrel dodged away. Blaze whipped around, kicked in the vicinity of the paint's jaw, and ran a few yards, then turned and neighed a challenge. The paint rushed in, and Ed winced as the crack of hoof on bone reached them.

~~~~~

"I don't like it." Jake paced back and forth in his front yard, from the captain's roan to where he had tied Rufus's horse to the corral fence. He'd ridden the boy's gelding out from the fort and had dismounted immediately when they reached the ranch.

"It's five miles, Jake," Byington said placidly.

"They ought to be here by now. Spook's faster than a flash flood in April."

Byington said nothing but watched the trail.

Iris saw that Laura was watching her father and her husband, knotting her hands in Shakespeare's reins. The two women had remained mounted so they could see better, and Iris's brother stayed near her. The trail was empty.

Iris sidled Tramp over next to Shakespeare.

"Laura, I'm scared."

Laura smiled, but the smile was troubled. "God is in control."

Iris nodded.

"I'm praying," Laura said softly.

"Me, too." Iris looked over to where her father, Zale, Pilcher and the other Mormon men waited. They fidgeted, too, and talked in low tones. Her father had seemed to stand on middle ground when he first arrived, but now he was definitely part of the Mormon group again. Conrad would do whatever her pa told him. She shivered as she realized she might be riding westward again soon. Very soon. She sent up another silent, desperate plea for Edward and her future.

At last Zale led his horse over to the captain's.

"You think something's wrong?"

220

"I don't know." Byington glanced at Jake. "Sherman seems to think so. Maybe they didn't start on time. I dare say they'll show up any second." He pulled out his watch.

"What time?" Jake asked.

"Twenty past."

Iris knew they had agreed that the riders would start at high noon, and Byington had set his watch by Coleman's.

"They should be here," Zale said.

Jake turned and strode toward the corral. "I'm not waiting any longer."

~~~~~

"I don't want to get between two stallions." Hal shook his head and held Lady steady as she pulled impatiently at the reins.

"That paint's got his band in the hills," Ed said. "I saw the mares for a second before I got to the stream. He thinks Blaze is invading his territory."

"Red will kill him." Rufus sounded doubtful, and he didn't meet the others' gaze.

"That mustang is tough as nails," Ed said. "Probably ran the old stud off and took over the herd. I've never seen them this close to the trail before."

The paint began to chase Blaze toward the pine forest, biting and slashing with his hooves. Blaze let out gasping cries and used his hooves to fight back, but he was giving ground, and his saddle had slipped down on the off side, until it was almost under his belly. Ed was sure the mustang would win.

"When Blaze has had enough, he'll light out for Utah," he predicted.

"Gotta stop him," Hal said. "I'm not chasing him clear to Echo Canyon again."

"Y'all back me up here, and maybe I kin get him," Riley drawled. He unhooked a rope from his saddle, and Ed took heart. The Texan spent his leisure hours roping fence posts and horses around the fort, and even pigs the supply sergeant raised for butchering. If anyone had a chance of catching Blaze, it was Riley.

He and Rufus could only watch in frustration as the troopers and Gluck fanned out, circling wide in an attempt to get beyond the dueling horses.

When Hal edged Lady up the hillside, the paint backed away from Blaze and whinnied sharply.

"You're heading in toward his band," Ed called. He wouldn't want to see the infuriated stallion turn on Hal.

Lady snuffled and fidgeted, and the mustang reared and beat the air with his hooves.

Riley began swinging a loop over his head. Ed watched in fascination, bouncing from one chilled foot to the other. *I gotta learn to do that.* If he could rope like Riley, he and Jake could catch a pasture full of horses.

Riley jogged his mount toward Blaze with the airborne loop circling. Blaze hopped toward the paint stallion and sank his teeth into his rump, and the paint squealed and lambasted him, his back hooves landing squarely on Blaze's chest. Blaze fell back, winded, just as Riley's rope snaked through the air, settling over his head.

The sorrel immediately began to plunge and fight the rope, then ran in close and kicked at Riley's horse. Hal and the other riders closed in, letting the paint slip between Hal and Gluck. He tore for the hillside, his hooves throwing up snow. Rufus ran forward with Ed limping along behind. By the time they reached them, Hal had Blaze's reins and was holding his head down, and Riley had his rope taut on the other side.

"Don't know but we should have had you rope the paint," Hal grinned at Riley. "Might make better breeding stock."

Riley spat on the ground. "This guy's purty, but he's not got the stuffin' that paint has."

They all looked toward the hillside. The paint horse was pounding toward the high mountains, his colorful tail flying.

"Hate to see him go," Ed sighed.

222

"Oh, you know it wouldn't be the same if there wasn't a wild stallion out there," Hal laughed.

Blaze stood panting, eyeing Riley balefully as the Texan eased his mount up close to the stallion's off side.

Rufus hung back.

"Get your saddle squared away," Ed said.

Rufus stepped forward timidly, and Ed sighed. "Oh, here." He pushed Rufus aside and pulled his gloves off, fumbling at the strap with fingers that were nearly numb.

"Let me help." Gluck dismounted and handed his reins to one of the troopers. He soon righted the saddle, and Blaze stood with his head down, trembling.

Gluck held out the reins to Rufus.

Hall called, "Mount up, boy, and finish your race."

Rufus scowled at him, and Ed knew he was afraid, but whether he feared the horse or his father's wrath more, he couldn't tell.

~~~~~

Jake and Andrew Byington loped out of the yard toward the trail. Zale and his friends were preparing to follow, and Jake wanted to be sure he was the first to meet the racers.

They had barely gained the wagon trail when he pulled Rufus's gelding to a halt. "Look."

Captain Byington stopped his roan, and they sat in silence for a moment, watching a gray horse pick its way toward them at a leisurely pace.

"It's Spook." Jake spurred forward, giving a whistle.

"Wait, Jake!" Byington rode up beside him.

"Something's happened to Edward!"

"I know, but you can't touch him."

"What?"

The captain laid a hand on his arm. "Let Spook come in by himself, son. We don't know what's happened yet, and he can't tell us, but you remember the rules we posted."

223

Comprehension hit Jake, and he nodded gravely at his father-in-law. "You're right."

Spook trotted up close and stopped, looking at him placidly. He snuffled and pawed the snow.

"Go home," Jake said.

Spook nickered and stretched out his neck.

"Git!"

"I'll go tell Laura," Byington said.

"No, if she calls him in, they'll say we cheated."

Jake wheeled his horse and loped back to the barnyard. The ache in his head throbbed with every step. Byington followed, and Spook trotted along behind.

Laura gasped when she saw Spook.

"Stay there," Jake ordered. He and Byington stopped their horses, and Jake held his breath as Spook trotted on past him.

Laura sat on Shakespeare well behind the finish line they had marked in the dirt.

No one said a word as Spook whinnied and shook his head, prancing up to Laura. She reached out and grasped his bridle. Jake exhaled in relief.

Laura looked at him anxiously. "Where's Edward?"

"What happened?" Zale demanded. "Where are Rufus and Red?"

"I don't know, but I aim to find out." Jake wheeled his horse and loped back out to the road. Captain Byington soon caught up with him.

"They're all coming, Jake, but I told Laura to stay put. She and Iris will take care of Spook. It looks like he's got a cut on his near hind leg and some bruises."

Jake grunted and urged his gelding to go faster. They cantered along the flat stretch to the edge of the pine woods before they saw anything out of the ordinary. As they entered the scrub growth, Jake reined in.

"Horses ahead. Get off the road. We don't want Rufus to run into us."

They pulled their mounts to the side as several horses appeared, trotting along the track through the pines.

"Looks like my men." Byington urged his roan forward. "Coleman, what happened?"

The soldiers trotted their horses forward to meet them, and the two groups came together in silence. Jake stared at his brother, who was riding double on Lady behind Hal.

"You all right?"

"Mostly." Ed saluted the captain and slid to the ground with a wince, and Lady stepped carefully away from him.

Jake looked beyond Lady to where Rufus sat, head down, on Blaze, then turned back to Ed. "All right, you're both safe. What happened?"

"Long story, brother, but in a nutshell, Spook and Blaze had a disagreement, and then that mustang stallion came along and picked a fight with Blaze. Spook up and left me behind."

Jake shook his head, unable to believe Edward had been unseated. He winced at the pain the simple action caused him. "There's more to it than that, I guess."

The Mormon men rode up quickly and halted, staring at the racers. Oscar Perkins was with them, but the young man, Conrad, had apparently stayed at the ranch with Iris.

"What's the matter with you, boy?" Zale snarled at his son.

"Let me through." Rufus guided the exhausted sorrel between the troopers' mounts and faced his father.

"I tried, Pa, but I almost drowned. I'm freezing to death."

Zale swore under his breath. "You take that horse and get to Sherman's, now!"

Rufus hesitated, then urged Blaze forward. The sorrel picked up a half-hearted trot.

"The race is over, Zale." Byington looked the bearded man evenly in the eyes.

"Young Sherman ain't finished."

"No, but his horse has. You're the one who came up with the wording. You didn't like our idea of a round-trip race, and we let you set the terms for the finish. First horse across the line at Sherman's ranch, you said, not first rider."

Hal smiled and patted the front of his wool coat. "I got the paper right here, gentlemen."

Zale pulled his rifle from his saddle scabbard, and Jake instinctively reached for his own.

"Don't even think about it, Sherman," Zale snapped.

Jake stopped with his hand in midair, but Coleman, Riley and the other three troopers had their sidearms drawn and pointing at Zale and his companions.

"Put it away, Zale." The captain's voice held the deep authority that brooked no resistance from his subordinates.

Zale looked around slowly. "I count the odds pretty much even."

Jake counted, too. Rufus was out of sight, but Zale had Pilcher and the other three who had ridden out of Echo Canyon with him the day before, plus Gluck and Perkins, who both had rifles on their saddles but had not yet drawn them. Seven guns.

He, on the other hand, had Edward, who was unarmed according to the race rules, Captain Byington, and five troopers.

Seven guns on each side. That's if he and the captain could draw theirs quickly enough. Should he try it? He knew he was the one Zale would aim for first. Probably Laura's father would be the next target.

Jake sat still, considering their chances.

Chapter 38

Blaze stumbled into the Shermans' dooryard panting.

"Rufus!" Iris ran toward him. "Where are the others? What happened to Edward?"

Rufus pushed the exhausted horse forward. "All you care about is Sherman. Well you'd better start caring about yourself, girl."

"What do you mean?"

Laura left Spook's side, where she had been washing the wound on his hind leg.

"Mr. Zale, did you meet my husband and the others?"

"Oh, yes. I met them, all right." Rufus was staring at the ground. "That the finish line?"

"Yes, but—"

He kicked Blaze, and the stallion crossed the line then stood with his sides heaving.

"There. I beat your precious Edward." Rufus slid over the side and dropped to the ground, staggering as he landed.

Laura's eyes sparked. "That may be so, but the rules say Blaze lost to my Spook, Mr. Zale, so don't expect any ribbons."

Iris watched her, terrified.

"Look at your horse!" Laura scolded. "He's shivering, and he's filthy. What did you do, roll in the creek?"

"Something like that."

Iris stepped forward and put her hand on Laura's arm. "Tell us, Rufus. Is Edward hurt?"

"I don't know. He was standing on his own feet when I left them all in the woods."

Laura looked at her, and Iris shuddered. "I want to go out there."

"No," said Laura. She looked toward the trail. "We'd better put Blaze in the barn and rub him down. I'll get you some coffee, Mr. Zale. You can get warmed up."

"Why aren't they here?" Iris rounded on Rufus. "You tell me now, Rufus Zale, or I'll tell your Pa you weren't really at Castle Rock that night you said you were."

Rufus's eyes widened. "You little witch!"

"Your pa will beat you," Iris said fiercely.

"You better not tell."

"What have I got to lose?"

Rufus stared at her, his mouth open, for several seconds.

Conrad had hung back during their exchange, but now he stepped up beside Iris. "You got a lot to lose, Zale."

Rufus gulped. "All right. All I know is, my pa told me to finish the race."

"Why didn't they follow you in?" Iris demanded.

"You'll have to ask him. Or your own pa. But I wouldn't count on spending the night here with your new friends. They might have other plans."

Iris stared into Laura's cloudy blue eyes.

"They'll be outnumbered," Iris said.

"Hal Coleman was going to come as soon as the race started," Laura said uncertainly.

Rufus said nothing.

"Please, Laura," Iris said. "We've got to go out there."

Conrad held out a hand. "Easy, Iris. It might be better to wait."

Laura nodded as though she had made her decision. "All right, we'll go, but we're not leaving Rufus here with the horses."

"I'll stay." Conrad sounded a bit uncertain, but Iris didn't blame him. He didn't want to be part of a confrontation. But still, he ought to be ready to stick up for his own sister, hadn't he?

Laura ran to the corral. "Quick, Iris. Take Blaze's saddle off. I'll catch Mabel, and Rufus can ride her."

"I ain't going," said Rufus.

Laura stopped in her tracks. She turned and smiled sweetly. "Do you want your coffee first, Mr. Zale?"

Iris couldn't believe she was willing to delay.

"Laura—"

But Laura was dashing into the house. Iris looked at Rufus with loathing. Was he deliberately keeping them here while his father executed the next step in his deceitful plot? He limped to the corral fence and leaned heavily on the top rail, watching the mares that moved about restlessly inside. "Coffee sounds good. See, Iris? That's the way a woman should behave. Think of the men first."

Laura catapulted out through the doorway holding her husband's Colt dragoon revolver in both hands to steady it. She aimed it at Rufus's chest.

"Saddle that red mare now, Mr. Zale. We're taking a ride."

~~~~~

Ed watched his brother, feeling helpless without a weapon. Jake was sizing up Zale and his cohorts.

After all we've been through, we can't let it end this way, Ed thought. The troopers were solid, every man. The captain wasn't wearing a holster, but he and Jake had rifles at hand. Ed edged closer to Riley's horse on his left. Riley also had a rifle, but had drawn his revolver instead. If lead started flying, maybe Ed could reach the rifle and help out.

He glanced up and caught Philip Gluck looking at him. Philip's face was unreadable, but it suddenly occurred to Ed that Gluck, who had supervised the start of the race with Coleman, was in a dangerous position. If he were to be counted with Zale's bunch, he was out of place, still sitting on his bay gelding between two of the troopers he'd ridden with from the fort. Philip had made a fair deal with Jake for some mares and had offered them hospitality. Would he turn on them now?

229

And what about Oscar Perkins? He, too, sat with his rifle still in the scabbard, a little apart from the others, a disquieted spectator. Ed drew a slow, deep breath. Assuming he survived, how could he face Iris again if her father were shot down?

"You can't think you'd get away with something like that," Byington said, staring at Zale.

"Why not?" Zale's smile turned Ed's stomach. "All witnesses will swear the truth—that you attacked us unprovoked."

Pilcher opened his mouth, then closed it.

Ed swallowed. He knew how the Saints had reacted when Johnston rode into their territory. He'd heard first-hand accounts of the destruction carried out by the Mormons on the army's supply wagon trains, and rumors of worse happenings.

"The U.S. government will never believe a story like that," he said, and all turned toward him.

"Not even when they learn you tried to carry off one of our women?" Zale's malevolent stare nettled him, but Ed stood firm.

"Leave Iris out of this."

"Oh, no. She's a big part of it." Zale glanced at Perkins. "I've spoken to her father today, Sherman. The Perkinses are coming back with us. You can just forget about any little schemes you been thinking of to steal my son's fiancée."

Jake shifted in his saddle but said nothing.

Philip Gluck pushed his horse forward a few steps. "Listen to me. Do you all really want to be blamed for a massacre? Well, I for one don't."

The Mormon men eyed each other uneasily. Ed was shocked that Philip dared to use the word.

Captain Byington looked from one man to another. "There's a lot of history here. We've got to learn from it, gentlemen. If you want to go seven guns against seven, think twice. My men are well trained in the art of war."

"Eight agin seven," Riley drawled, hefting his rifle and tossing it to Edward.

"No, nine against six," Philip said. He drew his gun and pulled back on his reins, until his gelding was once more in line with the troopers. "I won't lie against an honest man and steal from him. This whole dispute over the stallion is absurd." He nodded at Isaac Zale. "I saw the receipt you gave Thomas Sherman in my own kitchen. He gave it to his wife the night they stayed with us."

Zale scowled at him.

Philip repeated slowly, "I saw it."

"Watch yourself, boy," Zale snarled. "You'll regret this."

There was a commotion behind the group of Mormons, and three horses came into view.

"Father!"

"Laura, stay back," Captain Byington called.

"Is everything all right?" Despite her father's warning, she walked Shakespeare closer, and the men stared. Ed saw that Laura was holding Jake's revolver. Behind her came Iris, riding placid old Tramp and leading Mabel, and on the mare's back was Rufus, with his hands bound securely over the saddle's pommel. Ed's gaze didn't linger on Rufus, but slid back to Iris. She met his look, and he thought he saw a gleam in her eyes when she saw him.

"She's got my son trussed up like a turkey!"

Zale jerked his horse's head around, but Jake rode forward and grasped the gelding's reins just below the bit with his good hand. "Stay put, Mr. Zale."

Rufus sat miserably staring off to one side.

Laura shook her thick blonde braid back over her shoulder. "If this is a stand-off, Father, you have another gun here. You know I can use this."

Outrage distorted Zale's features. "Let go of my horse, Sherman!"

Pilcher timidly raised one hand. "It seems unwise to press the issue, Isaac. I think we should go."

Captain Byington nodded. "A good decision, Mr. Pilcher. Otherwise, my men might have to take Zale into custody for fraud and harassing the Shermans."

Zale looked stonily around at the others. Perkins met his look for a disconcerted moment, then looked away.

"You can stop at my place for the saddle that was on the stallion if you like," Jake offered.

Pilcher looked at Zale. "Perhaps it would be best to make that part of the deal, Isaac."

"No, we'll stop for the saddle and bridle," Zale growled. "Iris can get her things."

Iris gasped and looked toward her father. Ed felt rage welling up inside him.

"You got stuff at Miz Sherman's?" Perkins asked.

"Pa, you promised that if Spook won the race I could choose," Iris pleaded.

"He did come in first, Mr. Perkins," said Laura.

Perkins looked carefully at Pilcher and Zale, then back to his daughter.

Such a sweet, beseeching face would sway any man's heart, Ed thought. If he were Oscar Perkins, he would do anything to keep Iris safe and remove her from the harsh life she had led for the last few years.

Perkins cleared his throat and addressed the captain. "Would there be any use at Fort Bridger for a blacksmith, sir?"

Byington's features relaxed. "Yes, indeed. We have a man who shoes our remuda, but there's always more work than he can handle, and there's quite a village growing up around the fort, as you probably saw."

There was an awkward pause. Ed saw a look pass between Laura and his brother.

Jake raised his chin. "Let's put the guns away, folks. Everyone's welcome to stop for a bite at my house. My wife's handy at stretching a stew, and Rufus will need to thaw out before you head home."

232

~~~~~

"I wish the captain had sent some men with Mr. Gluck," Iris said softly. She still found it difficult to look Ed full in the face. When she did, her feelings rushed up like a flood, and she had to look away from the ardor that answered her in his eyes.

"Philip thought things would be all right, and Pilcher would tell the elders the truth."

"What if he didn't?" Iris couldn't help worrying about gentle Mary Gluck. She could be a hapless victim of this dispute, if Zale decided to wreak vengeance on Gluck for foiling his plans.

Four days had passed since the race, and they were sitting side by side on the bench near Jake and Laura's fireplace. It was Ed's first chance to get away from his duties at the fort, and Iris had had four days to wonder whether he would still feel as strongly about her when they met again as he had seemed to in the time of crisis.

Jake had prepared to go to the barn after supper to check the livestock, and Laura had teased him to take her along.

"We haven't had a moonlit walk for weeks," she'd wheedled. "Just let me get my coat."

"Mighty cold to be star-gazing, Mrs. Sherman." Jake had winked at Edward. "All right, sweetheart, we'll check old Spook's leg, but I'm sure he's going to be fine."

Iris knew Laura was conniving to leave her and Ed alone for a short time. There was little privacy in the Shermans' small home.

"The captain told Philip to come to the fort if he didn't feel safe," Ed assured her.

Iris sighed. "Do you think my pa and Conrad will be all right at Fort Bridger?"

Ed slipped his arm around her. "They're fine. I saw them this morning. The captain found them housing with one of the traders, and your pa's started working with the blacksmith already." His smile coaxed her to stop brooding. "Don't worry, Iris. Captain Byington was glad to find another man who could handle mules. Likely he'll get your brother on the payroll too, before long."

Iris lowered her lashes against the piercing power of his gaze. It made her stomach flutter, but she couldn't help smiling a little. "He was here Thursday evening to supper, but we didn't talk about you. I just ..." She let it trail off as she became acutely aware of Ed's nearness. He was drawing her closer tenderly, his brown eyes large and sober. She drew a quick breath and laid her hand against the front of his blue uniform shirt to hold him off. "Edward, I don't know how Pa feels about this," she whispered.

"He let you decide to stay."

"Yes, but—"

"And he decided not to go back, either."

"That's so."

"All right, I confess. I spoke to him this morning. I told him I was planning to come out here tonight to see you. He didn't seem to object."

Iris sighed and slumped against the warm support of his arm. She felt suddenly rich beyond every expectation, and warm and safe. She knew she could make her own future, and that was no longer frightening. She knew what she wanted, and Edward wanted that, too.

She sat straighter. "Ed, how am I going to tell him about God? I'm so ignorant myself. I tried to tell him that first morning, when he came to the fort, and look what happened! Because of my bumbling, he made you and Rufus race and put everyone in danger."

"It wasn't your fault."

She looked at him doubtfully, and he bent and kissed her right eyebrow gently.

"It really wasn't, Iris. But Jake and Laura and I will help you, and we're getting a chaplain this winter, so we'll have services, and you can learn faster."

Iris gulped. "Do you—would you—"

Ed was kissing her temple, and she found it extremely hard to think about what she was saying.

"Would I what?" His voice was so soft, it was a caress.

"Would you teach me everything you know about God?"

"Yes, of course."

She sighed in contentment. "Then I won't think about Pa anymore for now."

"Good." Ed turned her chin and looked deeply into her eyes. "Think about us now, Iris. I may not get another evening free for some time. But when I do, may I court you?"

She blinked. "I thought you were." His eyes crinkled in amusement, and she felt her face reddening. "Well, aren't you?"

Ed laughed. "Yes, sweetheart, I guess I am." He kissed her then, and Iris slid her fingertips up the front of his shirt, tracing the line of buttons to the collar, then slipped her hands around to meet at the back of his neck. Ed tightened his hold on her.

"Do you think that old stallion was worth it?" she whispered next to his ear.

He rubbed his scratchy jaw against her cheek. "Every penny. And every mile."

THE END

About the author: Susan Page Davis is the author of more than sixty published novels. She's a two-time winner of the Inspirational Readers' Choice Award, and also a winner of the Carol Award and two Will Rogers Medallions, and a finalist in the WILLA Awards and the More Than Magic Contest. A Maine native, she lived for a while in Oregon and now lives in Kentucky. Visit her website at: www.susanpagedavis.com , where you can sign up for her occasional newsletter and read a short story on her romance page. If you liked this book, please consider writing a review and posting it on Amazon, Goodreads, or the venue of your choice.

Find Susan at:
Website: www.susanpagedavis.com
Twitter: @SusanPageDavis
Facebook: https://www.facebook.com/susanpagedavisauthor

Dear Reader,

Thank you for choosing *Echo Canyon*. This story concerns a difficult time in our American history. Whether you agree with Iris and Ed's actions, I hope you have enjoyed the story.

My husband is descended from a line of Mormon pioneers, and when I was reading about their struggles, this book began to form in my mind. It's not the story of his ancestors, but they had episodes in their lives almost as exciting. His great-grandmother chose to leave the Mormon community and marry a non-Mormon in Nevada. I have great respect for her family's courage, hard work, and diligence in helping tame an inhospitable wilderness.

If you wish to review this book, that would be much appreciated by the author. You can view my other books at www.susanpagedavis.com and sign up for my occasional newsletter there or at https://madmimi.com/signups/118177/join .

If you liked this book, you may enjoy some of my other historical novels listed below.

Sincerely,
Susan Page Davis

Discussion Questions for Echo Canyon:

1. Iris felt she had no recourse in her situation. If you were in her place at the Whipple home, what would you have done? In the Zale home?

2. Laura Byington Sherman is unconventional for her time. What do you like about her most? Is there something you dislike about her?

3. If you were Laura giving Iris your New Testament, what passages would you urge her to read?

4. Iris is concerned for Betsy and Catherine's future. Should she try to contact Betsy after she leaves the Zale home? What do you think she could accomplish if she did?

5. What do you like or dislike about Ed's relationship with his brother? Laura's with her father?

6. Jake Sherman prefers his wife's nursing skills to the medical man at the fort's. Are there some things you prefer "homemade" instead of seeking out a professional?

7. How does Philip Gluck's presence complicate things during the race? He stands between two opposing groups. If you were Philip, would you have acted differently?

8. Iris is not ready to go back to living with her father and brother. Why not? What advice would you give her?

9. Did Iris steal the horse from Brother Zale? Is there another way she might have helped resolve the issue?

10. When he discovered the bill of sale was missing, Captain Byington reacted strongly. What should a man in his position do when something unexpected happens?

MORE OF SUSAN PAGE DAVIS'S HISTORICAL NOVELS
THAT YOU MIGHT ENJOY:

River Rest (set in 1918)
The Crimson Cipher (set in 1915)
The Outlaw Takes a Bride (western)
The Seafaring Women of the Vera B. (Co-authored with Susan's
son James S. Davis, set in the 1850s)
The Ladies' Shooting Club Series (westerns)
The Sheriff's Surrender
The Gunsmith's Gallantry
The Blacksmith's Bravery
Captive Trail (western)
Cowgirl Trail (western)
Heart of a Cowboy (western collection)
The Prairie Dreams series (set in the 1850s)
The Lady's Maid
Lady Anne's Quest
A Lady in the Making
Maine Brides (set in 1720, 1820, and 1895)
The Prisoner's Wife
The Castaway's Bride
The Lumberjack's Lady
White Mountain Brides (set in the 1690's in New Hampshire)
Wyoming Brides (set in the 1850s)
Love Finds You in Prince Edward Island (set in the 1850s)

Mystery and Suspense books by Susan Page Davis:
The Frasier Island Series:

Frasier Island
Finding Marie
Inside Story
Just Cause
Witness
On a Killer's Trail
Hearts in the Crosshairs
What a Picture's Worth
The Mainely Mysteries Series (coauthored by Susan's daughter, Megan Elaine Davis)
Homicide at Blue Heron Lake
Treasure at Blue Heron Lake
Impostors at Blue Heron Lake
Trail to Justice
And many more
See all of her books at www.susanpagedavis.com.

Sign up for Susan's occasional newsletter at
https://madmimi.com/signups/118177/join

CPSIA information can be obtained
at www.ICGtesting.com
Printed in the USA
LVOW12s1811150217
524373LV00004B/808/P

Echo Canyon

Copyright 2016 by Susan Page Davis.

Library of Congress Control Number: 2016920671

ISBN:
978-0-9972308-4-0